Alpha's Fated Flame

Omega for the Alphas: Fated Flames Book 1

Mina Summers

Contents

Content Guide   V

Omegaverse Terms   VII

Prologue   1

1. Chapter 1   6

2. Chapter 2   18

3. Chapter 3   29

4. Chapter 4   40

5. Chapter 5   51

6. Chapter 6   63

7. Chapter 7   74

8.   Chapter 8   84

9.   Chapter 9   94

10. Chapter 10   107

11. Chapter 11   117

12. Chapter 12   127

13. Chapter 13   138

14. Chapter 14   148

15. Chapter 15   159

16. Chapter 16   170

17. Chapter 17   181

18. Chapter 18   193

19. Chapter 19   202

20. Chapter 20   211

Epilogue   220

Thank you so much for reading!   224

Content Guide

If you don't have any triggers, please skip this page to avoid any spoilers!

<u>Trigger Warnings:</u>

- Torture/Violence

- Double penetration/ Backdoor Play

- Menage

- Somnophilia (mild)

- Claiming Bites

- Dubious Consent

- Mentions pregnancy and childbirth.

Omegaverse Terms

Alpha: Leaders of their werewolf packs. Usually in groups of three, four or five. Can only mate with omegas

Beta: Non-alpha wolves who live under the rule of their alpha leaders. They serve as the community and usually run businesses.

Omega: Special female wolves who only mate with alphas. They release certain scents that only alphas can detect. Born during an eclipse. Go through heat cycles when they find the alpha pack they are meant to mate with. Usually, they live in an omega nest until they are mated.

Omega Nest: A place where unmated omegas live until they find their alpha pack.

Heat Cycle: Omegas go through a period of intense sexual need that can only be relieved by multiple alpha knots.

Alpha Knots: Alpha wolves have penises in which the base swells up and locks into an omega, relieving her heat.

Slick: A secretion released from the genitals of omegas.

Rut: The term for the sexual needs of alpha wolves

Prologue

Adrianna

My hands shook as I grasped the envelope.

The letter was finally here, determining my fate if I belonged to my parents or if I was secretly switched out at birth. As I stood in my room, I could hear my mother humming along as she cooked dinner in the kitchen and the smell of fried meat in the air.

My nose wrinkled, hating the smell. I craved vegetables and fruit, the polar opposite of my entire family of werewolves. I surely didn't belong here.

Which was why I was holding this letter...

My heart pounded as I slowly opened the envelope, pulling the paper out.

Dear Adrianna,

Thank you for choosing Moon Clinic. We have run the DNA tests and can positively confirm that the mother and father cannot be excluded from the tested child. Based on this analysis, the probability of fatherhood and motherhood is 99.999%.

Thank you,

Moon Clinic

Breathing out a sigh of relief, I didn't know what I would do if my family weren't mine. And if I didn't belong to them.

I collapsed on my bed, which was on the lower bunk bed. My younger sister, Sarah, slept on the top bunk. She was hanging out with her friends after school. I had just gotten back from my college class, exhausted, as I crumpled the letter in my hand.

Even though I was nineteen, I couldn't afford to move out of my parent's house yet, though I desperately wanted to. I wanted some independence that I desperately craved.

The thought of staying out late partying without a constantly worried parent would be nice. To go on vacations without having to explain to them anything was my dream.

Two soft knocks sounded on the door.

"Come in," I called.

My mom, Melinda, walked inside, taking in my hazard appearance as I flopped on the bed wearing ripped jeans and a black hoodie. My long red hair had slipped out of its bun, framing messily around my face.

"You look tired," she observed, standing there with an apron wrapped around her chubby figure. She also had red hair like mine, but hers was jumbled in large rollers. "Your father is coming home soon. Do you mind helping me clean the kitchen?"

"Ugh," I muttered, closing my heavy eyes from exhaustion. "Just give me five minutes."

There was a sudden silence, and I opened my eyes to see my mother reading the letter from the DNA clinic. Oh my god, I wanted to get up and rip it from her hands, but it was too late. Her eyes widened as she scanned the letter.

"Why?" she gasped, looking at me in shock.

"I...I just wanted to know," I said lamely, slowly sitting up and feeling sick to my stomach that she discovered my doubts.

"But why? You don't think I'm your actual mother?"

"Because I haven't shifted yet," I admitted, staring at the worn blue carpet. "Maybe I'm human or something."

My mom sighed as she sat on the carpet before me, looking at me with concern and pity.

"Your day will come, my dear. You're a true werewolf through and through, just like the rest of us," she said in a low voice. Her hand rested on my knee. "For some wolves, it just takes a little longer. You belong in this family. Do you understand?"

I sighed, my heart heavy that I doubted she was my mother.

"I understand, Momma."

"I want you to let go of this obsession and just live your life as best you can. I want you to experience everything life offers before..." her voice trailed off as she bit her lip and looked away.

"Before what, Momma?" I said curiously.

"Before you get old and tired like me and your father," she said with a forced giggle. She quickly got up and made her way back to the kitchen.

I scrunched my eyebrows together at our exchange. I had a feeling that wasn't what she had wanted to say. She was hiding something and I could feel it.

Chapter 1

Two Years Later

Adrianna

"I think those guys would do," said my friend, Jess, pointing out a group of scraggly-looking human guys in the bar across from us. One of them was continually looking at me and winking.

I groaned.

"You're probably right," I said. "I think it's finally time to force my wolf to emerge."

"Remember, I'll keep watch from far away. If I don't see you shift, I'm jumping in pronto," said Jess. She was short but stubby and well-versed in karate. Her shoulders were hunched as she took a sip from her steaming coffee, watching the group of men.

"I don't think I can do this," I said.

"If you're serious about picking a fight with just anyone, I think I can handle them."

I didn't want it to come to this, but I had to take drastic measures now.

Waiting for my inner wolf to emerge wasn't going to happen on its own, and I needed to be in a life-or-death situation to trigger my shift. And tonight, I was intent on it to happen on my birthday, whether or not I liked it.

Jess knew about my death wish. Well, it was pretty much a death wish, and she wanted to take all the precautions necessary if anything went wrong.

"Do you think they'll try to attack a helpless lady like myself?" I said sarcastically.

"I think so," said Jess. "When they leave, try provoking them or something."

Was I doing the right thing?

Nervousness set in my stomach. The feeling of self-preservation came over me. I fought off that urge. If this is what I had to do to get my wolf out from wherever she was, then god dammit, I would do this no matter what.

She wouldn't be able to ignore me now.

"If I manage to shift..." I said, my voice trailing off.

"Then we're getting a huge cake tonight for your birthday and party like crazy," she said with a twinkle in her eye, a tendril of her blond hair curled over one eye.

Jess was a werewolf, and we grew up together, going to the same elementary school and college since our parents were close friends. I loved her to death. She was one of the few people aside from my family who knew of my unshifted status.

She wasn't an omega, and she greatly disdained them for some reason. I didn't hate any type of werewolf in particular myself. I just wanted to know if I even *was* one.

I never dared to casually date a werewolf, or else he might find out my secret. Not that I was even allowed around any other wolves besides my few friends. My parents never wanted me to be around the rest of the pack.

They claimed it was for my protection, to hide my secret of not having a wolf. Instead, they pushed me with enthusiasm towards the human world. But I was tired of living in isolation. I wanted to join the pack like everyone else.

And tonight, I was going to make sure that everything would change. I was going to shift tonight so I could attend the Were Gathering tomorrow with pride.

"Hey," I called to the group of guys as they rounded the corner of the bar when they left. I had followed them out leaving, and I was starting to doubt myself like I always did.

I pulled on my green shirt that matched my eyes perfectly, a little lower, showing off some cleavage. When they turned, my heart pounded like crazy. I felt like a fool standing under the night sky behind the bar, alone, as they gawked at me.

I knew Jess was keeping an eye behind one of the bushes, and that thought alone comforted me. *But what if she couldn't handle them and over-estimated her abilities?*

Oh god.

"Ooh, lookie here," leered one man, dropping his beer bottle and lumbering in my direction.

I licked my lips, my pulse racing as they surrounded me.

"She's hot," said another guy with stringy black hair, his hand on my shoulder. I didn't want them to actually touch me. Just to scare me enough so my wolf could emerge.

"Let go of me," I shouted, flinging his sticky hand off me.

His touch gave me the shivers.

His face twisted into rage as he grabbed my arm, pinning me to the concrete wall. I tried to punch him with my other arm, but a second man grabbed me, chuckling at my attempt.

Oh shit.

I tried to twist and turn out of their grasp, but it was useless. Their male strength was like steel to me. Unless I could shift, then I would have a fighting chance. Closing my eyes, I willed myself to shift.

Please, wolf, I begged in my head. I tried to imagine fur sprouting from my skin.

My adrenaline was through the roof when I felt their hot breaths on my neck.

Suddenly, I heard a loud bark, and the men immediately pulled away from me. *No! Jess was too early.* I turned my head to look at them, staring at the giant black wolf emerging from the shadows.

"Fuck," shouted one guy, and they all ran in the opposite direction, away from the wolf.

I stood there petrified. That wasn't Jess.

And if it wasn't Jess, then who the hell was it?!

The wolf barked again as he chased the lowlifes away from me. The muscles on his back flexed underneath his sleek, shiny midnight fur. Jess was running towards me, and the wolf immediately lunged towards her.

"No!" I screamed. "She's my friend!"

The werewolf backed away from her and turned his head toward where the guys went, sniffing the air. He was making sure they were really gone, and disappointment set in my belly as I looked down at my still-human form.

Jess grabbed my arm as we watched the wolf shift into his human form in the dark. I caught a glimpse of his massive muscular chest before he snapped a stretchy white shirt on and black pants he had left abandoned underneath the dumpster in his haste to save me.

I first noticed his golden irises as he walked towards me.

His long black hair lay messily around his shoulders as he gazed at me. I had never seen this alpha before in town. Even though I hadn't been around many wolves before, I knew he was alpha by his powerful physique and his alpha bark in his tone.

"He's fine," whispered Jess, also staring at him in awe.

"Stop staring so hard," I said under my breath.

He stopped in front of me, inspecting the bruises on my arms.

"What are you doing out so late?" he said gruffly while his fingers were wrapped around my arm.

I gulped.

My heart was beating a mile a minute at his touch. No man ever affected me the way he was doing right now. I knew Jess was smirking beside me from the side of my eye, but I couldn't help it. Warmth spiraled in my belly at his touch.

"I can be out late if I want to," I said. "But thanks for saving me."

His jaw flexed at my words. I knew I had hit a nerve there. Alphas loved to be in control.

"You're hurt," he said, his eyes fixated on my bruises. My skin ached with mild pain as he touched my arm. "You haven't answered my question. Why are you out so late?"

"It's none of your concern," I said, getting annoyed and pulling my arm away from him.

His eyes flashed at my attitude, and his lips thinned at my lack of respect. We weren't in the old days anymore, damn it. I didn't care, and I could feel Jess's shoulder shaking with laughter as she watched us.

"Why do you wish to die, foolish girl?" he asked, eyes flashing.

"Wow, minding your own damn business isn't really your thing, is it?" I retorted, stepping away from his grasp and pulling away from him.

What an arrogant prick...

He cocked his head to the side, the corner of his mouth pulling up as he looked at me with amusement. "That's fine. Next time, I'll let you die if that's what you really want."

"Damn right you should," I said.

"But for now, I am escorting you home. The streets are no place for someone like you."

I gasped as he pulled my hand in his, like a child, and started walking.

"Point me in the direction," he demanded.

I gaped at him, speed walking to match his long stride. Jess trailed along awkwardly behind us, as wide-eyed as me.

"My apartment is just around the corner," I sputtered out, finally finding my voice.

"Okay, I'll take you there," he grunted.

We rounded the corner and reached the steps of my old apartment. He released my hand and took a step back. He looked at me quizzically. "This is where you live?"

I had finally managed to move out of my family's house after there was no hope of me ever shifting, but I had to really downgrade to what I could afford with my cashier's salary.

"Yes, we can't all be rich alphas now, can we?" I snapped back, my hand fumbling in my purse for my keys.

I unlocked the door, and Jess and I stepped in. I quickly slammed the door in his shocked face, turning the lock.

Silence reigned over us, except for the beat of the music pumping from the neighboring apartment.

"Damn, girl. You told him off," whispered Jess as she pulled back the living room curtain. We both watched the alpha walk away in long strides. "An alpha out of all werewolves on top of that. You have some guts there."

Hot tears pricked my eyes, threatening to fall as the reality of my situation set in. I didn't care about that snobbish, overprotective alpha. I was upset that my mission failed miserably. I just wanted to be alone at this moment.

My body shuddered as the tears flowed down my face.

"I'll never be able to shift," I said. "I think I'm doomed to live a human life forever. I'll never be able to feel the wind on my face as I run..."

"Shh," Jess interrupted me, wrapping me in a hug. She patted my back as I cried awkwardly on her shoulder. She was a lot shorter than me. After a couple of minutes, I pulled away, hiccuping.

"Here's a tissue, Adrianna. Don't cry, okay? Your time will come."

"That's what everyone says," I said, blowing my nose into crinkled tissue from her pocket that smelled like mold.

"That alpha is probably so confused why you blew up on him," she said, and I giggled.

"Well, he messed up our plans," I said. "Didn't even give me a chance to fight the guys. I didn't even call for you yet."

"I know, but it probably wouldn't have worked anyway," said Jess.

"I think I'm going to head to bed now," I sighed. Today was a major disappointment.

"Why don't you come with me tomorrow to the Were Gathering," said Jess.

"You know I can't go," I said, shaking my head. "There will be way too many wolves there. I can't risk blowing my secret."

The Were Gathering was when all the packs in North America met up annually for games and challenges. It was supposed to keep us united from the ever-growing threat of humans exterminating us.

"You know what? Who cares?" said Jess. "You *are* a true werewolf. Being around lots of them tomorrow will be good for you, and who knows? It might trigger your wolf to emerge."

"Ugh, I'll think about it," I said.

"Good. I don't want to be around all those stuck-up omegas by myself."

Chapter 2

Kayden

What the fuck just happened?

I was bewildered as I strode away from that old, dingy apartment. Why was there an unmated omega wandering the streets alone at night? Did she have some crazy kind of death wish? She could have been kidnapped or sold by neighboring alpha packs living alone like that.

She should have been at home being pampered, perfumed, and prepared for tomorrow night's festivities. Not being manhandled by wasted humans in dark alleyways. She was at the mercy of anyone who came across her path.

I could have easily taken her away for my pack, but I would wait until tomorrow for the choosing of our omega.

Because we definitely needed an omega now.

And she was one of the most sexiest omegas I had ever seen. With mesmerizing green siren eyes and long, flaming red hair. And her scent... my cock was rock hard as I remembered it.

It was mouth-wateringly delicious, like hot drizzled caramel. Easily identifying her as an omega and different from other female wolves.

I really should have taken her for my own pack, and I was starting to regret it.

It was too late anyway.

I had already registered my pack for this year's omega choosing. I couldn't back out of it now. I didn't want to risk pissing off Roman and his hotheaded pack since they were hosting the Were Gathering this year. I wanted to make a deal to get in with his new lumber business.

I walked away from the rundown neighborhood and started making my way back to the mansion where my pack and I were staying. I have no idea why an omega was staying in this part of town. It was poor and dilapidated, unfit for her high status. And from what I just saw, the crime rate was through the roof. Plus, I could see that she had no survival instincts.

I remembered those bruises I saw earlier, glaringly stark against her arm's soft, delicate skin. That bothered me more than I cared to admit. My wolf's hackles were raised, and he still wouldn't settle down. I gave up the fight with my wolf, tore off my clothes, and let him out as I shifted again. He clawed at the earth and pointed his nose back toward where we came- to where the sexy omega was staying.

Nope, not happening.

I pulled the control back and turned us around to continue heading towards home.

The next morning, I pounded the punching bag conveniently provided in the mansion's gym.

"How about Grace Winters from the New Moon pack?"

Duncan, the second alpha of my pack, cleared his throat from beside me as he continued reading off of a list of omega names.

"Isn't she going into heat with the heirs of the Evergreen pack? I don't need to be making new enemies here, Duncan," I grunted while adjusting my right hook.

I landed another solid hit that sent the bag flying.

Sweat dripped down my forehead and into my eyes. I ignored it and kept pounding away at the bad. My muscles and my mind were nowhere near worked out enough. I was thinking too much about the omega from last night, and that was unhealthy if I was going to take on an omega today.

We were going to get the first pick of an omega because we were a powerful pack, the Bloodmoon pack. And no other alpha pack dared to challenge us.

Through my blood and sweat, I had carved out a place for my pack. This mansion that I had built for us and our future omega bride. At twenty-five, I had gathered and formed one of the most formidable packs in North America.

And now, at thirty-eight, it was high time I secured our pack's future by providing an heir or two. It was why I was officially searching for an omega to mate with me and the alphas of my pack.

It was unconventional, waiting this long without finding an omega to mate with. But I was ultra-focused on building up the strength of my pack for years. I found the strongest alphas to join in leadership with me. I gathered reliable betas with their families to build a powerful community.

And now all that was left was begetting heirs and continuing to build wealth.

Duncan sighed and adjusted his list, crossing off names left and right. He rubbed his hand over his short, brown buzz cut in frustration.

"You know what?" Duncan said.

"Yeah?"

"Roman is still offering to let you get the first pick at the drawing for the omega outings tomorrow. He claims it will make him more popular with the other packs. It's his hometown, after all."

"Our. Future. Is. Not. A. Fucking. Clown. Show."
I growled out, punctuating each word with a solid, bone-shattering hit to the bag. Somehow, it was still hanging on.

Damn. Really good quality.

"He's sweetened the deal."

I straighten up, interested now. I grabbed my water flask and chugged.

"Oh yeah?" I said, wiping my mouth, "How so?"

"He's offered the profit from the first two months of his new lumber business."

"Damn. Either he really wants this, or the fucker has money to spare." I mused.

Duncan chuckled, "It's no loss to us either way."

"No loss indeed."

I geared up, and with a final, powerful roundhouse kick, I knocked out the punching bag with a deafening bang, splitting it and strewing its contents out onto the floor. Duncan raised a thick, bushy eyebrow at the mess but wisely didn't say a word. He returned to flipping through the many stacks of pages around him.

Truthfully, it was an advantage to choose the omega you wanted. Usually, it was by the luck of the draw. You and your pack get matched. You go on a date and see if the omega goes into heat with you. If she does, she is yours to keep and mate with.

If she doesn't, you have to return her... fully intact without knotting her.

Still, I didn't want to seem like I was doing the fucker a favor. Roman and his pack just rubbed me the wrong way.

But what if that redheaded omega shows up in all her perfect glory...

Fuck, I needed to work out more. Clearly, my head was still not straight. Lucien, the third alpha of my pack, strode into the room briskly, his icy, pale eyes glinting in what I assume was irritation. With Lucien, it was hard to tell exactly what he was feeling, being that he was such a cold, emotionless son of a bitch.

His looks reflected his countenance, platinum blond hair, and freakishly near-white eyes. An ice cube in the form of an alpha.

An ice cube with a jagged scar running down the left side of his face.

"Kayden, we have a problem." He said, shrugging off his black jacket, revealing an impeccably ironed black shirt.

"What is it?" I said, grunting as I started on the weight machine, lifting at the max setting.

"It's Killian," Lucien replied solemnly.

"Yeah? What about him?" I snapped. "Spit it out unless you want to put on your pajamas and have a fucking sleepover about it."

Duncan let out a snicker behind me. I suppressed my own smirk.

I enjoyed baiting him for a reaction. And he enjoyed not giving me one. At least, I think he did. The bastard had no emotions. Lucien continued on with a poker face, as if I hadn't said anything at all.

"It appears he slept with three beta females who were all mated, and now their mates are calling for retribution. He claims he didn't know they were mated, and he's sitting in jail now."

I chuckled at that. Killian, the fourth and final alpha of my pack, had balls. I'd give him that.

"Help him out of that mess. The Were Gathering is starting soon, and we're not gonna miss it because he couldn't keep it in his pants."

"Will do," said Lucien.

Before Lucian turned away, I stopped him. "Hold on a minute."

I turned to Duncan as well, a pensive expression on my face. "This is going to sound weird, but have you guys ever heard of an omega living in poverty before?"

Duncan leaned forward, clasping his hands under his chin. "Nope, never heard that one before. Is this the start-up line to one of your jokes?"

"No," I sighed, "Unfortunately not."

Lucien looked directly at me and didn't beat around the bush. "What did you see, Kayden?"

"An unmated omega, living on the outskirts of town," I revealed. "She seemed to be on her own and clearly struggling."

"Why wouldn't she be living in a nest with the rest of the unmated omegas?" Duncan said, confused.

"Exactly, I was hoping to see her at the Were Gathering and get some answers," I replied. "Keep an eye out for her."

Killian

Ah, fuck.

I stared up gloomily at the dank ceiling above me, laying on a hard ass mattress, contemplating my life. It's not like I had anything else to do, seeing as I was locked up in jail at the moment.

I peered at the alpha bodyguard standing in front of my cell.

"Hey, man. Your pack unmated, too?" I asked him. He didn't reply, but I continued on anyway. "Shit, we're practically in the same boat. Why don't we let bygones be bygones and let me outta here? It's not like the beta guys can stop us."

He glared at me. "I don't work for no betas. I work for Roman. He says you gotta be locked up to keep the peace. Should have kept your dick in your pants."

I sighed and lay back down on the mattress. The pussy wasn't even worth all this trouble, now that I think about it. Especially beta pussy.

I heard a loud clatter of keys, jolting me out of my morose thoughts, and Lucien appeared at the door, unlocking it.

"Took you long enough," I muttered, getting up from the sorry excuse of a bed.

"Hey!" exclaimed the guard.

"He's free to go now. The betas received their compensation," said Lucien, cutting him off sharply. He turned to me and looked me up and down, noticing my ragged state. "Come on, get ready. We have a gathering to get to."

Chapter 3

Adrianna

I was in Jess's car as she drove us to the Were Gathering. My other friend, Amber, was sitting in the back, chattering away about her new beta boyfriend.

"We know he's hot and everything," sighed Jess. "But does he have *substance*?"

"Don't be mean," I laughed, sitting in the passenger watching the forest trees as we drove deeper to the secret werewolf location, away from prying human eyes.

"He does have substance!" said Amber indignantly. I saw her rolling her large doe-eyes from the rear-view mirror. She had long chestnut brown hair. She was a beauty but always had poor taste in men. The men could be good-looking, but her heart was constantly broken by them.

"I hope he's nice, at least," I said, fiddling with my thumbs. I tried to act upbeat and happy around my friends, but the truth was- I didn't want to go to this Were Gathering.

My parents had always drilled into me to stay away from other werewolves besides Jess and Amber. I felt nervous, defying the rule I lived by for so long. But my parents were right. I was probably better off living with the humans instead of exposing myself like this.

But it wasn't like my friends were ready to accept that. I vowed to make this my first and last werewolf outing.

"Are you still thinking about yesterday?" asked Jess, glancing at me. "I know that look. You're thinking of something, aren't you?"

"What happened yesterday?" asked Amber.

Jess explained everything to Amber while I sat silently, looking out the window and staring at the trees and nature.

"Oh my god, why didn't you tell me?" huffed Amber.

"You'd stop me," I said. "Anyway, it's not like it's going to happen again. I give up."

Then, in a softer tone, Amber tried consoling me. "Don't give up, Adrianna. You're a true werewolf."

"I know," I said, after hearing this same thing for the millionth time. It was the exact reason I hated talking about this to everyone. I was hoping Jess wouldn't out me, but it wouldn't be fair to Amber since we were all friends.

"Looks like we're here," said Jess, to my relief, parking on the side of the road behind a long line of cars. The GPS was blank on the dashboard, with no signal, which meant we were right where we needed to be, where the humans couldn't find us.

As we exited the car, I inhaled the sharp scent of pine trees - the cool breeze hitting my face. It was a beautiful fall day, and it felt good to be away from my cashier's job for a bit and take a break. I worked as a cashier at a gas station.

It was the best I could do for myself. I had dropped out of college last year when I decided it was just too expensive and I couldn't keep taking out student loans.

I took a deep breath before we entered the camp.

The huge bonfire was already roaring as we approached the campgrounds. Two alpha bodyguards stood at the entrance of the curved gates, waiting for us. They sniffed us as we walked by them, and they put out an arm to stop us.

I was freaked out by that since that never happened to me before.

"Hold on a sec," one of them said gruffly.

He looked at me strangely, up and down, at my casual outfit. I had worn a simple pair of jeans and a black crop top that showed off my midsection. Then, he had me write out my name on a little slip of paper that they threw into a hot pink jar.

"What's that for?" I asked.

"It's for the drawing later," he replied, puzzled at my question. Jess and Amber shrugged, looking confused as well. They weren't asked to put their names in, and I wondered what was so special about me. Oh well, they'll find out soon enough that I was probably human.

There were about three hundred werewolves lounging around. The females were chatting away, and the males flexing in front of them. Fully shifted werewolves prowled the grounds, keeping watch.

My eyes widened at the sight. It looked like it was a highly organized event. I could see wild dancing, drinking, laughter, and speakers discussing werewolf pride and the evilness of humans.

Now, I wish I had put a little more effort into my outfit especially when I glanced at the high stage in the center of it all.

On the stage, lounged about a dozen or so beautifully dolled-up females on soft, plush cushions and pink fur rugs. They had bowls of fruit and candy strewn about as they giggled amongst themselves. They shyly peeked out from behind handheld, bejeweled fans with kohl-rimmed eyes.

My jaw dropped at the display.

"Are those the stuck up omegas you were talking about?" I whispered to Jess.

"Yup," she replied grimly. "They think they're better than the rest of us, since alphas can only mate with them and not betas."

"Well, they *are* very beautiful," I said, looking curiously at a stunning blonde omega dressed in red silks, who was winking at every alpha male walking by the stage.

She noticed me staring and held my gaze. She dropped her flirty act and gave me a small half-smile tinged with sadness. She looked away and resumed her attention towards the alpha males.

"That's because they get the best resources at the expense of the rest of us. God, I can't stand omega wolves," growled Jess, her nose high in the air as she turned away from the display.

At the moment, she looked more stuck up than they did.

I spotted my family standing in front of the bonfire, my mother talking to my sisters, Sarah and Lacy. My dad was throwing more wood into the fire and smiling at what they were saying.

"Oh shit," I ducked quickly behind Jess, trying to hide myself from their view. Amber was long gone with her new beta boyfriend.

"What is it?" Jess said loudly, trying to turn around to see me.

"No, Jess," I hissed at her, "It's my parents. They'll kill me if they see me here. You have to take me back home now!"

She sighed and walked towards a refreshment table so I could duck behind it and be out of view from my family.

"Girl, we came here to have fun, so we're gonna have fun. Screw it! Who cares if people find out you don't have a wolf?"

I opened my mouth to argue but was suddenly cut off by Jess's fangirl squealing.

"What?" I asked, irritated, looking to where her gaze was set.

"Oh my god, look, Adrianna! That's Roman, the alpha of our pack," she said, blushing uncontrollably. "It looks like he's about to make a speech."

I got up tentatively from behind the table to look at the stage before us. I saw a tall, blonde man holding the microphone, tapping into it to test the sound. He reminded me of a Ken Barbie doll.

"Welcome, brethren," he started, and the crowd slowly quieted. "I have a quick announcement before we begin our festivities."

"Ooh," said Jess in my ear as we listened.

"The powerful Bloodmoon pack will join us today for our annual gathering," Roman announced. "The alphas, led by Kayden, are searching for their one true omega. And as he is one of my closest friends, I have agreed to grant him first choice in the pick for the omega outings!"

Kayden walked up to the stage, and I gasped when I saw his face. Jess and I exchanged shocked looks. It was the same alpha from last night who marched me home.

Three alphas joined him, standing in a row behind him. Roman held out the pink jar I had mindlessly thrown my name in earlier.

"Now, would you like to pick randomly from the jar of names, or did anyone already catch your eye?"

Wait, what the hell?

Didn't he say they were looking for an omega? Then why did they ask me to put my name in that jar? I turned to Jess.

"Is this supposed to happen? I think my name is in that jar."

She bit her lip, confused.

Just then, I felt a hot prickling feeling on the back of my neck. I turned back towards the stage, and my eyes collided with Kayden's hot golden gaze.

He lifted his hand and pointed straight at me.

"We want her," he announced loudly. Suddenly, all eyes were turned to me. I heard a shriek from the crowd.

It was my mother. She looked at me with horrified eyes.

"Adrianna! No! What are you doing here?" She said. Then she turned the stage and shouted. "No, you're mistaken. She's not an omega!"

I stood frozen in place.

No way this was happening. At my elbows appeared the two alpha bodyguards from earlier. They grasped my arms and started frog-marching me towards the stage.

"I'm not an omega," I said over and over, trying to pull away.

The walk was a blurry haze, and suddenly, I was in front of Kayden. I looked up at him and found he was already staring at me with a dark, heated gaze. I glanced away towards my mother, who was still shouting and pleading, tears and mascara running down her face.

"Don't take my daughter!"

The crowd started rumbling, the confusion causing restlessness and agitation. My heart was racing a mile a minute.

Roman stepped towards me, inhaling deeply. Kayden let out a protective growl, putting his body between us and shoving me back towards the group of the three tall alphas. Immediately, they circled me, and I stared at a wall of muscle.

Through it, I heard Roman trying to keep some semblance of peace.

"This girl smells like an omega. She will remain with the Bloodmoon Pack until she goes into heat with them. And from now on, she will follow the rules expected of her as an omega," Roman announced. "Settle down everyone."

"Please, I'm not an omega, though," I pleaded, trying to remove myself from this mess.

Kayden turned to the giant of an alpha in front of me, the one with a military buzz cut.

"Duncan, take her back to the house. I will stay back and smooth things over. Killian and Lucien, make sure the crowd can't get near her."

I heard affirmative replies, and the wall of muscles started moving. I moved my feet, to stay in the protective bubble as we entered the now rowdy crowd. People tried reaching in to get another glimpse of me, but we moved through swiftly, heading to what I assumed was the car.

As we passed the omega stage, I caught a glimpse of the blonde I had seen earlier. She looked at me with pitiful compassion and mouthed. "Good luck."

Chapter 4

Adrianna

I wanted to get as far away as possible from this gathering. I had enough for the night and just wanted to get home and forget all this happened. This was all just a cruel joke, as if I could ever be a contender for being the mate of alphas. I wasn't supposed to ever have an alpha mate.

I wasn't an omega, and I felt sick to my stomach.

My heart felt like it was shattering into a million painful shards. Unexpected tears pricked at my eyes. I thought I was all cried out years ago, but every day brought fresh reminders of how different I was.

We reached the gate that separated the clearing from the parking lot. I was almost out of this nightmare of everyone staring at me. The human-hybrid freak show. In my rush, I bumped into the solid mass in front of me. I lost my balance and started to fall.

Suddenly, I felt large hands wrapping around my waist, steadying me from falling. My skin tingled and warmed at the touch, and I looked up directly into the icy gaze of the most striking alpha I'd ever seen.

My eyes widened, taking in the sight of his pale hair and eyes. But most of all, I noticed the jagged scar running down the left side of his face, destroying the cold perfection.

Our bodies were inches away. I could feel his breath on my cheek. His arms were steel rods ensuring my safety, and I could feel the strength of his muscles.

I couldn't move away.

Something was changing in me; something was different that I couldn't quite place. A heat was emerging from my core and radiating out all over my body. I couldn't quite catch my breath.

41

Warmth pooled in my body, and deep inside me, something stirred.

What is wrong with me? Was I sick?

I parted my lips, my breath coming out in quick gasps. Only mere inches separated my lips from his. And this man's lips were the only soft part I could see of his body. They looked tantalizing and cooling. A cooling I desperately needed as the heat in my body reached a fever pitch.

My clothes felt itchy and uncomfortable. My jeans were way too rough, rubbing on the skin of my inner thighs. My bra straps felt two sizes too small.

I just wanted to rip everything off and let the cool night air relax me.

What was going on? This wasn't me. These feelings were alien and invasive.

Shocked at myself, I pulled away from his arms. I saw a knowing, hurt disappointment flash in his eyes before he quickly masked his expression and turned his face away. He resumed his brisk walk, and I was confused by all the feelings he arose in me.

Lucien

Bitterness coated the back of my throat.

For a minute there, I had hoped that maybe this time might be different, that maybe I could be near a beautiful female without her shivering in disgust. But she was no different from all those other empty-headed females. Only seeing my scar first and not the alpha behind it.

I quickly resumed my mask, the emotionless face that kept everyone away at arm's length. Exactly the way I preferred.

Fuck. Her scent was so tempting, a warm caramel that matched her long, red hair perfectly. The complete opposite of me. She was warm and soft when I held her, the warmth of her skin lingering on my hands.

We reached the car, and I quickly opened the car door for her. I averted my gaze, staring off into the distance so I wouldn't have to endure any more disgusted looks from her. But to my surprise, she completely ignored the open door and started walking away from us.

Killian and Duncan exchanged confused glances. I sighed. She was probably a spoiled rotten omega who didn't want to follow our lead.

"I got this," I said to them. She just needed someone to fear to keep her line. I guess it was up to me to play that role.

I quickly caught up to her and grabbed her elbow.

"And where do you think you're going, little omega?" I growled into her ear, inhaling her sweet scent. She turned to face me and hit me with the full force of her green-eyed gaze.

There wasn't a hint of fear in them.

"Thanks for getting me through that crowd, but I'm gonna head back home now," she said sweetly.

I raised my brow. *Was she serious right now?*

"Yeah, that's not happening. You're an omega. We won you fair and square, so now you belong with us until tomorrow to determine your fate," I drawled out, pulling her body closer to me.

She peeked up at me through thick, black lashes.

God, she was cute.

She scrunched up her nose and opened her mouth for a retort. I didn't give her the chance. I picked her up and threw her over my shoulder, and I placed one hand firmly over her ass to keep her in place.

I gave it a warning squeeze when she let out a shrill scream.

From the corner of my eye, I could see some curious stragglers from the crowd trying to approach us. We needed to get out of here. I slid into the leather seats in the back of the car and placed the sputtering omega on my lap, clasping her firmly.

Duncan was already in the driver's seat, with Killian beside him. They shot the omega curious glances, as stunned by her beauty as I was.

"Let me go," she shrieked. "You don't understand. I'm not an omega. I'm not who you think I am."

I rubbed her plush bottom over my hard cock. I knew she could feel the thickness of it through the layers of clothes between us.

"You feel that, little omega? You are exactly who we think you are. Here's your proof."

She fell into a mortified silence, her cheeks turning an adorable shade of pink. She nervously licked her lips and tried again in a calmer voice.

"Listen, there must have been some mistake. I'm just a college dropout and a gas station cashier. I'm not a part of your world for a reason."

"And what reason would that be?" I said distractedly, playing with her caramel-scented hair. I put my nose to it and inhaled deeply. I couldn't get enough of her scent.

She chewed her bottom lip and looked away, nervously clasping her hands together. "I can't tell you, but if you could just drop me off at this light, I can find my way home."

I stopped playing with her hair and put a finger under her chin, tilting her pretty face up towards me.

"The sooner you stop resisting, the sooner we can tell whether or not you're going into heat with us. Stop resisting, little omega, and relax."

Her body slumped against me in defeat. "I have a name, you know."

"Oh, yeah?" I replied, trying hard to focus on the conversation and not thinking about tearing off her clothes to get closer to that caramel scent.

"Yes, it's Adrianna," she said primly as if we were in some board meeting.

"And I'm Lucien," I said, licking up the side of her neck, giving up the impossible fight. She squeaked and tried pulling away from me. "Why do you taste so good little omega?"

She was breathing hard with panic, and I could sense her emotion changing to fear. I quit licking her neck and instead settled her more firmly over my hard cock.

"What's going to happen?" she asked with fear in her voice.

"Hey, there's no need to be scared," I said. "If we're your true mates, you'll go into heat, and we will do the honor of knotting you."

Her cheeks turned a delicious shade of pink, and I grinned.

Adrianna

The pale alpha, Lucien, refused to listen to a word I had said during the car ride. I blushed, remembering the way he had held me and licked me in the car. I felt hot all over and gladly welcomed the privacy of the room they had shown me to.

We were in some sort of giant mansion, clearly on the better side of town. I could hear muttering outside the room door, but I didn't care. I had closed and locked the door without another word to any of those alphas.

They couldn't admit that they made a mistake bringing me here. They were probably too prideful. I heard alphas could get that way. So, I guess I'll be stuck waiting until tomorrow to play by their stupid rule, and then I would be free to go when they discovered I wasn't an omega.

But it didn't mean I had to see them in the meantime.

Was the freaking air conditioning on in here? My thighs were damp from the heat. You would think a fancy place like this would have good air conditioning. I walked further into the room and saw a small shower in the bathroom.

Perfect.

At least I could cool off there. I peeled off my clothes, struggling to pull off my now-damp jeans. I hopped in and turned on the water to the coolest setting. I shivered as the cool water hit my body, but I still felt burning hot from within.

What the hell was going on? I stayed there for a few more minutes until my stomach started cramping from the cold water. I sighed and got out, drying off with a towel. Another wave of cramps hit my stomach, and I let out a whimper.

I looked around but didn't find any clean clothes to wear. I didn't want to wear the same clothes I had on before as I hung my wet jeans over a chair.

Oh well.

I let the towel drop to the floor and climbed into the massive bed in the center of the room. I slid, naked, into the beautiful, soft red bedsheets.

This place was exquisite, nothing like I had ever seen before.

I would have enjoyed this experience if it weren't for the whole kidnapping part. I clenched my teeth together as my stomach balled up on itself again. I wish I had some pain reliever medicine with me right now.

I had cramps before, but this pain was on a whole other level. My body was clamping down on itself while my skin was heating. I felt the moisture between my thighs again.

Was I bleeding?

I lifted the sheets but couldn't see any blood. Since arriving here, I didn't eat or drink anything, so it couldn't be drugs.

I lay on my side and held a fluffy pillow against my belly, which did little to relieve the pain. I made myself as comfortable as I closed my eyes, attempting to drift off to sleep and get this night over with.

Chapter 5

Kayden

After settling the crowd, I arrived at the mansion and found all three of my pack standing in front of what I assumed to be the omega's room.

"What's going on?" I asked.

"Adrianna locked us out," Killian replied, grinning devilishly.

Hmm...Adrianna, I thought, pretty name.

Duncan walked towards me and pulled me to the side. "I think she's gone into heat already. I can hear her in pain, and I smell her scent through the door."

I raised my brows, shocked. That was fast.

"We didn't even spend much time with her," I said. "Has anyone been messing around with her?"

Lucien grinned. "I sat her on my lap and played with her a little. That must have brought her heat on so early."

"Does that mean we get to keep her?" asked Killian.

"Hold on, we need to do this right. Duncan, why don't you go in there and break the news to her? You're the nicest of all of us, and we should make a good impression."

"She's under the impression that she's not an omega, and this is all a big mistake," Duncan replied grimly.

"Alright, fine. I'll go in," I said. I didn't trust myself around Adrianna while she was in heat. I might scare her off completely.

I reached into my pocket for a spare key and unlocked the door. I entered the dark room, closing the door behind me. I walked to the bed and saw her sleeping in the center of the bed.

She was sleeping fitfully, tossing and turning and whimpering in pain. Her forehead glistened with sweat. At one point, the bed sheet slipped down, revealing one pale, luscious breast.

Oh fuck. My cock jerked at the pretty display. She was most definitely in heat. I inhaled deeply, smelling her slick from where I stood, and the urge to rut came over me. My cock tented my pants as I sat down on the bed next to her.

I slowly reached over and cupped her breast in my hand.

She didn't stir, so I moved my fingers, playing with her exposed pink nipple. I lowered my head, sucking on it deeply. She moaned in her sleep and turned her body towards me instinctively. I dragged down the sheet, freeing her other breast to play with. Goddamn, she was so fucking sexy.

With my other hand, I reached under the sheets and found her legs already splayed wide open, her naked, wet pussy freely accessible to my touch. And it was dripping wet with her slick, ready to be knotted. But I needed her awake for that, especially for our first time.

I played with her clit and watched her face, her sleep much calmer now than when I had first walked in.

Adrianna

I kept my face completely relaxed, and my eyes closed. I didn't move a single muscle. At first, I thought I was dreaming, seeing the shadowy blur of a figure seated next to me.

Then, I noticed the sensations happening between my legs. A hand stroking my clit, a mouth sucking on my nipple, and then I knew I wasn't dreaming. I didn't want to open my eyes; I wanted it to continue. My cramps were noticeably lessened but still there.

Then his finger slipped into my pussy.

My eyes shot open, and I stared straight into the hot golden gaze of the alpha who had saved me last night, Kayden.

"It's nice to meet you, Adrianna," he said, not missing a beat as if we were in a coffee shop. He inserted a second finger in my pussy, thrusting in and out, slick coating his hand.

"It's nice to meet you, too," I breathed out, cheeks burning with embarrassment at the smacking sounds coming from between my legs. But it felt so good. I needed more.

My pussy clenched down on his fingers, needing some-thing more filling. He chuckled and thrusted faster.

"What is going on?" I wondered out loud, moaning with pleasure.

"You're going into heat. You need our knots to stop your pain," he said, strumming my clit with his thumb.

"Our?" I asked, confused. Then I looked up, and around the bed stood three more alphas, all staring directly at my exposed pussy with heated gazes and tented pants. I squeaked in mortification, slamming my legs closed and pulling up the bedsheets to cover myself. My belly clenched in disapproval.

"What the hell is wrong with you guys?" I yelled out, the haze of pleasure dissipating.

One of them stepped forward, the one with the brown buzz cut and burly frame. He held his hands soothingly as he sat on my other side.

"Hey, Adrianna. Look, I know you're scared and prob-ably confused, but this is completely normal. You're an omega, and it seems like we are to be your pack since you're in heat right now. We can take away the pain if you let us."

Oh my god, they really believed in their delusion. Logic wasn't going to work here.

"No offense, but I don't even know you guys, and you don't know me," I said, trying to make him see reason.

"You're right," he replied. My heart leaped with hope. Finally, I could get out of here.

"Good," I said.

"My name is Duncan, and I believe you already met Kayden and Lucien. And he's Killian." He pointed to the tattooed alpha, who was staring at me hungrily.

"Okay, thank you for the introductions. Now, if you could just please get me some pain meds and a phone, I'll be okay," I said, gritting my teeth at the returning pain in my belly.

Duncan and Kayden exchanged looks over my head.

"Alright, Adrianna. We'll get you what you need. Just remember that we are here to help you," Duncan said calmly.

I groaned out my reply. The cramps were coming back with a vengeance.

They left the room reluctantly, and someone brought back a bottle of meds and a cell phone. I didn't bother opening my eyes fully at this point. It hurt too much. I blindly reached over and grabbed the phone.

I squinted out of one eye and dialed my mother's number. She answered before the first ring could even finish.

"Momma, it's me," I whimpered out.

"Oh, Adrianna! What did you do? I told you never to attend the Were Gatherings," she said hysterically.

"I don't care about my wolf secret, Momma. Something else is wrong with me." I said, cutting her off.

"It was never about your wolf! We hid you because you're an omega. You were born during an eclipse, but we hid you so you would have a chance at your own life," she revealed hurriedly.

My mouth dropped open.

What the hell?

Were those alphas not delusional after all? I felt like a fool. But why wouldn't my parents tell me who I truly was? My heart shattered at her betrayal.

"I'm an omega?"

"Your wolf didn't show up because you were never around any alpha males to trigger your omega hormones," she said, sobbing into the phone.

It felt like a knife twisting into my heart. All this time, I could have been normal, and part of a pack. I wasn't defective or broken. Tears streamed down my face, and I angrily swiped them away.

"How could you let me believe I was broken? All this time, you knew what I was and didn't tell me," I said, my voice shaking with emotion.

"I'm sorry, Adrianna! I wanted you to have a normal life," she cried.

"Well, it's not up to you to decide," I said bitterly, hanging up the phone.

I cried out as another wave of pain hit me stronger than before, my insides clenching up on emptiness. I wiped away the rest of my tears and swallowed down the pain meds. The conversation with my mom kept replaying over and over in my head.

I can't believe my parents knew all this time and didn't even bother telling me. I felt like I lost a part of my life that

I could never get back. So many nights wasted, crying over something that could have been easily fixed. How could I ever forgive my parents for keeping a part of me secret from even myself?

I needed a distraction until the pain meds kicked in. I called out softly, "Duncan?"

The door opened almost immediately, and he came barreling in, a box of tissues in hand. I giggled softly despite my tears and sadness.

It was obvious he had stayed by the door this whole time. My heart warmed at his thoughtfulness. He reminded me of a cuddly bear with a calm, centered energy.

He handed me the box and sat down next to me. He stroked my messed-up hair while I blew my nose. Suddenly, he pulled me into his lap, encircling me with his giant arms. I stiffened at first but then gave up the fight. It felt nice to be held like this after the turbulent emotions lately.

"What's wrong, Adrianna?" He asked me softly.

"I just feel like my whole life was a lie, you know?" I replied quietly. The shock of the truth was wearing off. In its place was a yearning for something to put out the fire blazing in my core.

I peeked up at him, gazing into his warm chocolate eyes. Being around him put me at ease. Something about his large presence made me feel safe. He smiled down at me and then unexpectedly captured my mouth with his lips.

I closed my eyes, moaning. It felt so good compared to the sadness I had been feeling earlier. He parted my lips with his tongue, kissing me deeply and thoroughly. His hands played with my hair and roamed my bare back. I shivered deliciously. His touch was feathery light.

Then, he gripped my naked legs, opening them and turning me so I could straddle his lap, and we were face to face. With our height difference, I was more at his chest level. He leaned down and kissed me, slowly exploring my mouth.

I couldn't wait anymore. My pussy was drenched with slick and throbbing with need. He sensed my urgency and pulled down his pants, his massive cock springing free. I gasped in shock.

I felt suddenly unsure of myself. I never had sex before, and his dick looked obscenely large. I felt nervous, but my body was built for this, built for an alpha cock. At least I knew this interesting fact about omegas. I took a deep breath, and I looked up at Duncan with wide eyes.

"Is this your first time, love?" He asked me gently, his calm demeanor at odds with his large, angry-looking member. A drop of pre-cum slipped down the side of it. I nodded dumbly, at a loss for words. His eyes softened, and he held me close. "Don't worry, love, I'll take care of you."

His hand reached down between us, and he played with my clit, relaxing me. My legs fell open further, and I thrust my pussy into his hand shamelessly.

I had been close to the edge for far too long now, and I needed relief. He chuckled and withdrew his hand. I mewled in frustration. But then, with one swift movement, he lifted me up and then impaled me fully down on his cock. I gasped at the tearing pain, tears stinging the corner of my eyes.

He kept perfectly still and resumed his attention on my clit. Slowly, the pain faded. He whispered comforting

61

words in my ear and kept strumming my clit lightly. Then, in its place, a delicious fullness emerged.

His cock was fully embedded in me, and slick was running down my inner thighs freely. It felt so damn good. My pussy walls contracted on his hard, full length, finally stuffed with what it had craved.

Chapter 6

Duncan

I felt so honored Adrianna had chosen me to be her first, above the rest. I took that role seriously, and I would damn well make sure she had a good time. I yearned to thrust and move inside her tight channel, but I held perfectly still, letting her adjust to my size.

Her caramel scent filled my nose as I held her close. Then she lifted herself up off my cock and kissed me open-mouthed. *Oh fuck.* My restraint was at an end. I grabbed her hips, positioned her, and brought her firmly back down on my cock, stretching her tight pussy to its limits. She threw her head back, moaning.

I guided her, showing her how to ride my cock, and she was a fast study, bouncing up and down with ease. The room was filled with the sound of her wet pussy sliding up and down my cock. She came all over my dick, moaning deeply, releasing more slick and clenching me hard with her pussy walls.

I couldn't hold out anymore and came with a growl, spurting hard deep inside her. Her channel milked me for every drop, squeezing my cock. I filled her up with my hot liquid. Then the base of my dick swelled hugely, locking us together with suction.

She gasped, "What is that?"

"It's my knot, love. This will help you with your pain. But you're going to need more than one knot since you're still in heat."

She bit her lip and looked away. "I don't think I could do that. You're fine, but the rest are..." her voice trailed off nervously.

I hugged her close. My heart melted with sadness, remembering the way I found her in the room. She was clutching the phone with a lost expression on her face, the bedsheet wrapped loosely around her. I had to comfort her and make her feel loved. And now I needed to soothe her fears.

"I'll be with you the whole time. This is what your body needs. The pack will take care of you just like how I did," I told her.

She looked down at our joined bodies, where my knot still joined us together, and her face turned an adorable shade of red that matched her hair. I wanted to laugh, but I held it to avoid hurting her feelings.

She chewed on her bottom lip. "Well, the pain is completely gone for now. Maybe I don't need their knots after all."

I sighed. This wasn't going to be easy.

"Omegas usually go into heat for like a week or so. You want to stay ahead of the pain so it doesn't get that bad again. This is supposed to be a pleasurable time for you," I said, trying to explain the process to her.

She didn't reply and tried pulling herself away from my knot and winced in pain.

"Why can't I go?" She asked in confusion.

I looked at her in wonderment. She had no idea what it meant to be an omega. It seems her parents hadn't told her a single thing about the world she was from. It would be up to us to teach her.

"Until my knot goes back down, we are stuck together. Trying to leave will only cause you pain," I explained gently to her.

She huffed in annoyance and stared off into the distance, awkward and silent. I looked up at the ceiling, studying its pattern.

Damn, this just turned really awkward.

Adrianna

When Duncan's freakishly large knot went down, he quietly exited the room after our awkward exchange. I wasn't excited at the prospect of getting knotted like that over and over again. I hopped back into the shower and scrubbed myself clean. As the water washed over me, the ache between my legs seemed to calm down the longer I stood under the water. After my shower, I found a dress lying on the bed with the tags on it. Someone had obviously gone shopping for me.

I held it up; it was a cute sunflower yellow dress. It was the complete opposite of anything I would ever wear. I looked around but couldn't find any underwear to accompany it. I slipped it on and walked towards the window.

Sunlight was streaming into the room, the horrid night a distant memory. My stomach growled with hunger. I hadn't eaten since going to the gathering last night, and I was starving. Especially after my recent activities, I thought, blushing.

Between my legs was a lingering pleasant ache, and the horrible cramps did not return. My thoughts turned positive that maybe everything would be okay. I took a deep breath and fortified myself with courage. I walked to the locked door and hesitantly unlocked it. I needed to find food quickly before I fainted.

No alpha came barreling through, so I released the breath I was holding and tentatively opened the door, peeking into the hallway outside. No one was there, but my nose was hit with the smell of delicious eggs and baked goods. My heart leaped at the thought of finally eating.

I followed the yummy smell and went down a huge flight of stairs. I rounded the fancy corner and heard the chatter of male conversation coming from what appeared to be the kitchen. I stepped into the room, and all four alphas fell silent, gaping at me.

Kayden was the first to recover, swiftly pulling out a mahogany chair at the dining table. "Good morning, Adrianna. I trust you're feeling better now?"

I nodded slowly and sat down in the offered chair, my cheeks burning. It was pretty obvious everyone knew what me and Duncan were up to earlier. But my hunger quickly overrode my embarrassment as I glanced over at the stove. I raised my brows at the sight.

Killian stood over there with a black apron on, managing four skillets at once. He expertly flipped pancakes, scrambled eggs, and roasted potatoes effortlessly. He even reached into the oven and pulled out a delicious-looking coffee cake.

I did not expect the tattooed alpha to be so talented in the kitchen. He caught me staring and winked at me with his roguish grin. "Like what you see, darling?"

I blushed harder if that was even possible. Kayden assembled a giant plate of food and set it down in front of me with a cup of coffee.

"Eat," he said. "You'll need your strength to get through your heat." I raised my brow at his commanding tone, but I was too hungry to argue. The food smelled so good and tasted even better. To my surprise, I cleared the whole plate and looked for seconds.

After satisfying my hunger, I looked around the room at the four very different alphas. The problem wasn't that I didn't find them attractive; it was that all of them turned me on, and that freaked me out. I didn't feel normal craving for four guys at the same time.

I grew up mostly in the human world, where everyone was strictly monogamous unless they were cheating scumbags. Having more than one partner was considered a bad thing in my mind. I guess I would have to work on uncoupling that from my current situation.

My belly flipped at the thought of having all four of them in bed. Slick gushed out of me, and I squeezed my legs together quickly, mortified. I had no underwear on. Lucien slowly put down his fork and turned his head towards me, inhaling deeply. Oh shit, he noticed.

"Looks like someone enjoyed her breakfast," he said in his gravelly voice. I looked into his pale eyes, and my pussy clenched, releasing more slick.

"Fuck," he said, abandoning his food and getting up from his seat. Killian tore off his apron and came over as well. I shot up from my seat and held up my hands, backing up.

"Hold on, guys. This isn't happening," I said warningly. I backed up some more and bumped into someone behind me. I felt hands at my hips, and I turned and saw Kayden holding me, his erection visible through his pants.

I turned back around and bumped into Lucien, who stood equally close. I almost wanted to laugh and cry at my current predicament. I was sandwiched between two very horny alphas. My pussy throbbed, but I wasn't having it.

I just couldn't get past my hang-ups over sleeping with multiple alphas.

"Look, I get that I'm an omega now, but I'm not into the whole four guys thing, okay? It's no offense to any of you..." my voice trailed off as Kayden started kissing my neck. Lucien reached over and started massaging my breasts through the very thin sundress.

My eyes fluttered shut, and I moaned, losing my train of thought.

"You need to turn off your thinking, baby," Kayden said against my neck, nibbling and licking. Lucien pulled down the elastic front of my dress, exposing my braless breasts. He sucked and fondled them.

Now I see why this particular outfit was chosen for me. Everything was easily accessible for everyone, I thought, scandalized.

Killian wasn't about to be left out. He faced me towards him, keeping Kayden to my right and Lucien to my left, and kneeled down at my feet. I looked down at him in confusion until he lifted one of my legs onto his shoulder, giving him a clear view of my pussy.

The dress hid nothing from his sight, especially since I had no panties on.

I gasped, but before I could say a word, he latched his mouth directly onto my clit, sucking deeply. Kayden had his hot mouth on one of my breasts, licking and plucking at my sensitive nipple. Lucien sucked at my other breast, stroking my neck with the back of his hand.

I felt a strong, steadying presence at my back, bracing me. It was Duncan, ensuring I didn't fall. I felt his hard erection pressing against my bottom. Clearly, our session this morning was not enough for him. I gave up the fight and let my head fall back onto his chest, moaning deeply with pleasure.

I didn't care if this was morally wrong or not; it felt so damn good, and I was tired of fighting my body. I would analyze and overthink it later, but for now, I wanted to relax and be knotted by these sexy as hell alphas.

Killian inserted two tattooed fingers inside my channel, hooking it and massaging my inner walls. He unlatched from my clit to rasp out, "You like that, darling?"

"I do," I gasped out, "Don't stop, please!"

He sucked my clit back into his mouth, rubbing my g spot until I screamed with pleasure. I came all over his hand, gushing slick. But the pleasure was short-lived.

My belly started clenching with pain again.

Oh no, I had waited too long without a knot. I doubled over and cried out. Kayden picked me up into his arms and made his way to the stairs.

"Don't worry, baby, we got you. We'll take away your pain," he said soothingly, walking up the long flight of stairs.

The others followed him as we made our way back into my room. Kayden laid me down on the bed, and the others joined us. The massive red bed easily held all of us.

Chapter 7

Adrianna

This scene was so different from the nightmare of last night.

At that time, all I could think about was getting away from the crazy alphas and getting home. Now, I wouldn't want to be anywhere else in the world.

All four of them gazed at me in adornment, and I wondered at my luck. I went from being lonely and isolated in the world to being surrounded by more alphas than I knew what to do with.

I was being stroked and petted by all four of them.

In this moment, I had never felt more desired and treasured in my life. They were treating me like I was precious gold. I sat with my back against Kayden's chest, encircled by his magnificent presence.

Out of all the alphas, I felt his raw energy the strongest. He was a force to be reckoned with, a true leader in every sense of the word. He reminded me of a lion, a king of the jungle.

Killian continued eating me out, my legs spread wide open for the view of the alphas. I groaned as another spasm hit me. Kayden quickly released his cock from his pants, and I felt the hard length against my back.

"Almost there, baby, I got what you need," he rumbled into my neck. He lifted me up, and everyone could see his massive cock entering me, inch by glorious inch. I moaned in relief, my pussy spasming helplessly against his hard length.

All three of the remaining alphas had their dicks in hand, watching my pink pussy swallowing their leader's dick over and over. My breasts bounced shamelessly as

Kayden accelerated, thrusting in and out with gusto. I cried out, slick dripping out of me.

Suddenly, my moans were cut short as Killian brought his long cock to my lips. He smoldered me with his hot, devil-may-care gaze.

"Open up that sweet mouth of yours, darling," he coaxed me gently. I opened wide, and he slid his dick deep into my mouth.

Every time Kayden bounced me on his dick, it shoved the cock in my mouth deeper and deeper. I swirled my tongue along Killian's length as best as I was able. I felt helplessly spit-roasted between two alphas.

Kayden held my hips down and, with a last thrust, spurted deep inside me. His huge knot swelled up instantly, locking us together firmly. He stroked my clit softly as I continued sucking Killian's member.

I felt on top of the world, having one of my alphas locked inside me and the other deep in my throat. My pain was gone, and all I felt was extreme contentment. I can't believe I had fought this fate for as long as I did.

Killian groaned and released his seed straight into my mouth. I looked him in the eye and swallowed every last drop, making sure to lick his dick clean. I released it from my mouth with a pop, and he leaned down and kissed me thoroughly.

I felt the knot go back down and release me from Kayden's cock. I turned to him, and he claimed my mouth next, exploring it deeply with his tongue.

Lucien

I watched the little omega get fucked, and it took everything in me not to come right then and there. She was so goddamn beautiful it hurt to look at her. But now it was finally my turn. The other alphas stepped away from the room, understanding my need for privacy. Then, it was just me and her left in the room. The sexy omega, all spread out and flushed from head to toe. Perfection.

She looked at me with an adorable, heated gaze in her eyes. The scar on my face throbbed under her curious look, and I fought the urge to look away, to hide my shame. Many women had cringed away from me before I even opened my mouth to speak. But she gazed at me with a boldness I had rarely seen with anyone besides my pack.

I approached her slowly to not startle her and sat down beside her on the bed. I reached over and touched her hair. I couldn't help bringing it to my nose to inhale her delicious scent. I could not get enough of that caramel perfume she emitted. She giggled and licked her lips nervously, her pink tongue darting out. My balls tightened, aching for release.

A gasp cut her giggle short, and she clutched her stomach as her heating cramps hit her hard again. She looked at me with wide eyes in pained confusion.

"Why is it coming back so soon? I just had Kayden's knot?" She asked me, puzzled.

"You're in the thick of your heat, little omega," I told her, stroking the side of her face. "You'll need your entire pack's knots to help you get through this."

She leaned into my touch, fluttering her eyes shut. Good. With her eyes closed, maybe she could forget my disfigurement and imagine someone else was fucking her.

Now that she wasn't looking at my face, I unleashed the restraint I had. I allowed myself to capture her lips with mine, kissing her deeply. I kneaded her perfect tits, enjoying how she moaned into my mouth.

I reached a hand down between her legs and felt her release slick into my hand. She blushed and immediately pulled away from me, her eyes downcast, avoiding my gaze.

It felt like a knife in my chest. There it is, the disgust. She didn't want me touching her. She would rather have someone else from the pack. I shifted, getting ready to get up and leave, but her whisper stopped me in my tracks.

"I'm not clean down there. You shouldn't touch me there," she said softly, shame burning her cheeks. I felt sucker-punched with shock.

Shame was an emotion I knew all too well. And this beautiful omega should never have to experience anything even close to shame. I looked at her in stunned shock, and she blushed harder, avoiding my gaze completely.

My heart softened.

She wasn't rejecting me at all. She misguidedly believed she wasn't worthy of me. That was the furthest thing from the truth. It was almost laughable. But first things first. It was time to take care of her, to show her how much more worthy she was than me.

"Come here, little omega," I growled.

I lifted her up in one swoop, and she squealed in shock. I walked to the tiny bathroom and deposited her down gently into the shower. I turned on the water and adjusted the temperature before I let the spray hit her body.

I quickly removed the rest of my clothes and hopped in with her into the cramped space.

I looked her in the eye and cupped her soft cheek. "You are never dirty to me. I don't want you to ever feel that way."

She looked up at me, blinking the water out of her eyes, and breathed, "Okay."

She twined her arms around my neck and pressed her naked, wet tits against my chest. I groaned and couldn't wait any longer. My balls were about to burst, remembering her sexy display earlier.

But I couldn't fuck her while she was facing me. Every woman I had ever had sex with requested to face away from me so they wouldn't have to endure seeing my scarred appearance. I was used to it by now, and it didn't bother me anymore.

"Turn around, little omega," I told her.

She furrowed her brow in confusion. "What do you mean?"

"I'll show you exactly what I mean," I said, the anticipation making my dick leak out some droplets of precum.

I turned her around to face the wall and spread her legs wide open. She was short, so it took a little maneuvering, but eventually, I got my dick between her legs and rubbed up against her slippery pussy.

She pushed her perfect ass back and let my dick push into her hole. "Oh fuck, little omega." I wasn't going to last long with the way she was teasing me.

I slowly pushed inside her, watching my dick get enveloped by her pink folds. She cried out against the shower wall as she got stuffed, once again, with an alpha cock.

I wrapped my arms around her to cup her tits in my hands and roll her nipples between my fingers. I thrust into her steadily, establishing a rhythm. She matched that energy by pushing her hips back as far as she could. My balls slapped against her clit, and she shivered with delight, squeezing my dick as she came over and over.

I roared out my release, holding her ass tight against me as I pumped my seed deep inside her womb. My knot swelled large, locking us together and ensuring not a single drop of my cum spilled out.

She sighed in contentment, leaning back to rest against my chest. I reached over, grabbed some soap, and started lathering up her already glowing skin. We were still locked together, but I did my best to clean every inch of skin I could find.

"How did you get your scar, if you don't mind me being nosey?" She asked me idly, chasing water droplets with her finger.

I froze up, the soap bar dropping from my hand with a thud.

Images flashed in my head of dark closets and whimpering. A large man's hand grabbing me... My breath came out in short pants, and I knew I needed to get away from here as soon as possible.

"What happened?" she said, trying to turn and see my face. Mercifully, my knot went down, and I quickly withdrew from her body with a sucking sound. She gasped at the abruptness of suddenly being empty and bereft.

I felt bad, but I had to leave to get my head straight and my emotions back under wraps where they belonged. I hopped out of the shower and left the bathroom, answering none of her probing inquiries.

Chapter 8

Adrianna

What the hell was that all about?

I wondered at the abruptness of Lucien storming out as I continued to lather myself up with soap. The rejection stung a little after the amazing experience we had just shared. Well, it actually stung a lot. Tears pricked the corner of my eyes, but I dashed them away with the water.

Yes, my question could be considered a little rude and invasive, but I thought we had a connection. I forced myself back into the present moment and shook off my ill feelings. I wouldn't let one bad moment taint an entire day of wonderfulness.

It didn't even feel like a day. It felt like I had been with these alphas for a lifetime. There was this bond that I could not explain, connecting me with them and making them feel like the family I had always longed to be a part of.

I finished washing myself up and turned off the water. I scanned my belly for any sign of pain, but I was good so far. Fingers-crossed that this was the end of my heat. Although, aside from the pain, it really wasn't a hardship to be in heat.

I smiled to myself, feeling the pleasant ache between my thighs as I walked back into the bedroom. I found another dress lying down on the perfectly made-up bed. This time, it was a shade of green that matched my eyes perfectly.

It was also as provocative as the former dress I had worn. I slipped it on, the buttery fabric feeling wonderful against my skin. I left my room, looking for some company.

I found Duncan sitting in what appeared to be a library. Stacks of books surrounded him, and he was scribbling away in some notepad. I sat down across from him at the table. He looked up and flashed me a warm smile.

"Hello, love. I'll be done soon, and then I can come and find some food with you."

His calm greeting soothed my heart from Lucien's cold exit, and I smiled happily back at him.

"There's no need. I don't want to bother you. I was just wondering where everyone was at."

"They went out to finish up some more pack business before we head back to Nevada," he said matter-of-factly.

My heart stopped.

"You guys are leaving?" I asked in a pained whisper. I had already gotten attached way too fast. *What the hell was wrong with me?*

Duncan looked up at me sharply, but then a knowing realization came over him. "You really don't know what it means to be an omega, don't you?"

I huffed in annoyance. "And I'm really tired of hearing that."

"Obviously, you are coming with us, love. We are your pack now, and we are to be together for the rest of our lives," he explained carefully.

I balked at his words. "Look, this was fun, whatever this was. But I'm not about to leave my hometown to go shack up with four dudes," I said, trying to remain calm. "If you guys want to stay in town, we can date or something."

"So you're planning to raise our pups on your own?" He inquired, raising a thick brow.

His words were like a bucket of ice-cold water splashing onto my face. Pups?

Adrianna, you fucking fool.

The thought of pregnancy never even crossed my mind. All this time, I was gallivanting about with zero form of birth control. I clutched my stomach in horror. I was way too young to be a mother and literally just met these alphas.

"This is a good thing, love," he pressed on. "After all, this is why Kayden wanted to find our mate. He needed pups desperately."

That was the final nail in the coffin...my heart shattered into a million painful shards.

"So this whole time, I was just meant to be an incubator for your pack?" I asked in a pained whisper.

"No, love, don't say it like that," he said, trying to backtrack quickly. His face twisted like he knew he fucked up big time. "Of course, after we met you, everything changed."

I felt like vomiting. I stood up and held out a shaky hand to stop his desperate ramblings. "I heard enough, Duncan."

"Where are you going?" he asked tentatively.

"I'm hungry. I'm going to go make a sandwich or something," I said- the lie springing from my lips with ease.

"I can help you with that," he said, getting up from his seat.

"No, no," I said, forcing a giggle. "I just need time to process my new life, and I'd like to be alone."

Before he could say another word, I spun on my heel and left the library. I ran back to my room and grabbed the phone they had given me and the credit card that I had come in with. I raced down the stairs and into the familiar kitchen. I looked around and spied the key rack I had half noticed the last time I was here.

I rushed over and grabbed the first set of car keys I could find. I only had a limited window of opportunity before the rest of the alphas returned. I was getting the hell out of here, and something told me they would never let me go.

I carefully opened the side door and eased my way outside. I didn't want to alert Duncan that I was leaving the premises. Even though he was only one alpha, I knew without a shadow of a doubt that he could easily keep me here if he knew I was escaping.

I closed the door behind me and raced to the front of the house. My heart was pounding a million miles a minute. I clicked the remote on the car key like a madwoman until I saw the car flashing in response. It was a nondescript, small, gray car.

Absolutely perfect.

I hopped in and turned it on, wincing at the sound of the low humming engine. I looked up at the front door, but Duncan did not come barreling out. *I was going to make it.*

I drove out of the unfamiliar area until I hit the main road. I sighed in relief. I knew where I was now. Jess's house was not too far away. I could lie low and stay with her for a while. Eventually, the alphas would have to leave town, and then I would be free again.

I chewed on my lower lip nervously.

I placed a hand on my belly. There was no way I could be pregnant already. *But the chance was still there.* I hushed the little voice in the back of my head. I would deal with that if that were to happen. But for now, my focus was on myself and my freedom.

I pulled up to Jess's house and took a shaky, steadying breath. I got out of my car and made my way to her front door, ringing the doorbell. The door opened immediately.

"Adrianna? What are you doing here?" She asked, stunned.

Seeing a familiar face after the tumultuous time I experienced melted my heart.

"Oh, Jess," I said, reaching in for a hug.

She pulled away in disgust, and I stood there, arms outstretched like a fool.

"You're an omega," she spat out hatefully.

"Jess, what the hell is wrong with you? It's me, Adrianna," I said, hurt beyond belief.

"I'm not friends with any omegas. Why don't you go back to your pampered little palace and leave me alone?" she hissed with narrowed eyes.

"You're such a hateful bitch. You have no idea what I'm going through," I yelled at her.

"And you have no idea how omegas treated me like I was trash," said Jess.

"I would never treat you like that. You know me."

She just sneered at me, her face a frozen mask of revulsion. I turned away and ran back to my car, slamming the door and driving off. The tears poured down my face freely now. I had nowhere else to go. Jess hated me on sight, and my family lied to me for years.

I was on my own now, and I had no idea what I would do.

Shit, I was out of gas. The gas icon was lit up at 11 p.m., and I had driven for miles at this point. I had left town ages ago. I yawned and rubbed my tired eyes. It was probably a good time to stop and sleep for a while.

I had successfully disappeared. I didn't know whether I should be feeling relieved or devastated.

I pulled into a nearby gas station I spotted. There were only three pumps, but that was okay. No one was there anyway at this time of the night. There was even a cute little hotel nearby that I would definitely check out.

I hopped out of my car and popped the gas tank open. I took out my credit card. Pangs of sadness hit me as I swiped it onto the machine. As the gas started gurgling into the car, I leaned back against the hood of the car and stared up into the night sky.

It was a beautiful moon out tonight, a full one. Out here, in the middle of nowhere, I had no one to distract me from my lonely thoughts.

Suddenly, a huge white van came barreling into the gas station with blinding lights and blaring music. It halted with a screech. A human man spilled out, swaggering and cursing at himself. He looked unkempt and scruffy. The smell of old cigarettes and booze wafted over to me.

I gagged at the scent.

I shrank into the side of my car, hoping to make myself as inconspicuous as possible. But it was too late. I had already been spotted.

Chapter 9

Adrianna

The man came lurching over to me. He wore tattered, dirty clothing with greasy, unwashed hair. He wiped at his mouth with the back of one hand.

"Whatcha doin' out here all by your lonesome, little gal?" He grunted out.

I remained silent and quickly pulled out the gas pump and closed the valve with shaking hands. I was painfully aware of my lonely state with no one knowing of my whereabouts.

The man grew irritated at my silence and drew even closer. He slammed his hand on my car door just as I was opening it and slammed it shut. My heart pounded in my throat. I nervously fluttered my hands. I had no idea what to do.

"What's the matter, cat got your tongue?" He continued slyly, "Or should I say wolf?"

I stopped breathing.

Was this a human who trafficked and sold wolves as experiments in human labs? We had all grown up hearing about those stories of the poor, unfortunate wolves that get kidnapped and tortured into pieces, all in the name of science. We were warned young to avoid these type of humans and situations.

And here I was, smack dab in the middle of one.

"I have no idea what you're talking about," I squeaked out.

He laughed derisively. "I know your kind well. What with you starin' up at the moon like that? You ain't nothin' but a goddamn freak o' nature wolf."

He pulled out a switchblade and flicked it open near my face.

"Hey, hey, hey!" I started exclaiming. "Look, I don't want any trouble. You can have my credit card if you want."

The man grunted and looked at me with one squinty eye. He slowly closed the switchblade, purposely in my line of sight. "Credit card, eh?" He said thoughtfully.

"Yes," I cried desperately. "You can have it if you just leave me alone."

Then, as fast as a snake, he raised his fist towards my head.

Oh god!

That was the last thought I had before the world went black.

Pain...

Blinding pain.

That was the first coherent thought that came to me as I slowly gained awareness again. The back of my head was pounding, a horrible stabbing pain. It felt like a knife was being rammed into my skull repeatedly.

My eyes remained shut, but I became aware of movement. The rumbling vibration of a moving vehicle.

I slowly opened my eyes. The first thing I saw was my bound hands in front of me. A thick rope was wrapped around over and over again and tightly knotted. The same went for my legs. I tried to open my mouth, and to my horror, it was taped shut.

I tried blinking away the pain to take stock of my situation. I was alone in the back of a vehicle. There was a black mesh partition in front of me. Dividing the driver and passenger seats from the rest of the vehicle.

Wiggling my fingers proved to be futile. I could not loosen the ropes even an inch. My bladder slowly started increasing its alarm. I needed a bathroom fast. I grunted through the tape as loud as I could, but the engine of the van drowned the sound out.

Eventually, I lost the fight with nature and relieved myself where I sat. I silently sobbed with the humiliation.

Tears streamed down my face, and my nose ran freely. There was nothing I could do about it.

As if he could hear my thoughts, the driver turned around and grinned at me. I choked on the remnants of my tears. It was the creepy human from the gas station.

Oh shit! I was so dead.

From what I could tell through the little window high up in the van, we had been driving all night, and dawn was approaching. My mouth was bone dry, and my stomach was rumbling. I shifted my legs, uncomfortable in the sticky wetness of my dress.

Even prisoners were allowed to use the toilet. This guy was treating me like the animal he believed me to be. Oh, if only he knew he hadn't exactly captured a real, functioning werewolf. I was just an omega who had never been around enough alphas to trigger her wolf.

The van came to a sudden stop, and I lurched forward on my face onto the dusty floor filled with suspiciously sticky substances. I gagged through the tape. My hands were useless to brace me from the fall.

The van's sliding door opened with a rusty screech. I turned my head to the side as best as I could to see what was happening.

The man appeared in the opening, holding up a flashlight, a slobbering grin on his face. He looked as if he had captured a prized fish or hunted a large stag. He was looking through me, not *at* me, which made this whole thing even creepier. He had already dismissed me as a lesser creature than him in his mind.

"Okay, okay, next we have to get it into the barn," he muttered gleefully as he checked over the tightness of my ropes. I watched him with horrified eyes.

What the hell was about to happen to me?

Satisfied, he grabbed me by my bound hands and started dragging me out of the van. I hooked my bound feet onto the door and silently screamed through the tape. I wiggled, trying to escape his grasp.

He grunted, "Dumb bitch!"

He let go, breathing heavily through his nose, and slanted his piggish eyes angrily. He pulled out a heavy wooden bat from under the seat and quickly smashed it onto my right kneecap.

I let out a bloodcurdling scream, muffled almost completely by the tape. I went limp; the pain horrific. It felt like my leg was snapped in two. Tears streamed down my face.

He giggled to himself and continued dragging me out of the van. I hit the pavement, sharp stones digging into me. I barely registered that pain. My leg was an all-consuming fire of hurt.

I was dragged down a long driveway. Eventually, we reached the barn door he was muttering about earlier. I silently screamed the whole way there. My shattered kneecap was scraping against the pavement with every step he took.

He searched his grimy pockets for the key, found it, and inserted it into the lock with his stubby, sweaty fingers. The door opened, revealing a dismal room filled with random piles of hay. I could only see a couple of feet further than the doorway. The rest of the room was shrouded in shadow.

The stench of old blood and rotting carcasses hit me in the face.

I shuddered. I could not see in the dim light where the stench was coming from or whether it was emanating from all around.

The man pushed me inside and grabbed the thick iron shackles that were mounted onto the wall. He didn't bother removing the ropes from me and clamped the shackles wherever he could. And without another word, he scurried out and slammed the door shut, engulfing the room in darkness.

At first, I could see nothing. The darkness of the room and the blinding pain in my leg made me oblivious to my surroundings.

But then, slowly, my eyes started adjusting. The pounding in my leg faded into a dull, constant throb in the background, matching the ache in the back of my head. Tiny rays of light trickled in through the small gaps of the slats in the walls and ceilings. I could tell where the room began and ended.

I could also make out some misshapen lumps strewn about the room.

I pulled on the shackles and found I had some slack to maneuver somewhat without jostling my leg. Bracing myself with my forearms, I dragged myself to the nearest lump. At first, I could not process what I was seeing, then I tried so hard to scream with horror through the tape covering my mouth. But only grunting noises came through.

It was a werewolf, or what was left of him. A pile of distorted, broken limbs, fur, and skin. There were missing pieces and parts, but the body was mashed together like a broken puzzle set.

I quickly dragged myself back to my original spot, sobbing.

That's it. This is where I die.

A brutal, slow, torturous death. All alone. I closed my eyes for a long time, imagining myself anywhere but here. More than anything, I wanted to be back with Kayden and his pack. Living with them and having their babies sounded like paradise compared to where I was now.

I was so goddamn stupid for taking off like that.

Warm, yellow sunshine made its way through the gaps in the slats, warming my face and calming my thoughts. I opened my eyes. For a minute, I could believe that everything was okay. Sunlight had a way of cleansing the bad and making you think only of the good.

But even the sunlight was not enough this time to erase the horror I was in. My stomach no longer rumbled. I was accustomed to the lack of food now. I felt dizzy from the pain and weakness in my body.

As if on cue, the barn door opened, and the horrible man slithered in. He still wore the stained, dirty clothes he had on from the first time I saw him. I guess hygiene wasn't as important to him as torturing werewolves.

I almost let out an inappropriate snort.

He had in his hands a doggie bowl of water. My eyes were drawn to it. My tongue felt heavy and thick in my fuzzy mouth. I needed it so badly. He placed it down in front of me, just out of reach. He also laid out the tool belt he had wrapped around his waist.

"Okay now, what should we get started with?" he chuckled to himself as he surveyed his tools.

I dry heaved in my mouth. I knew what was coming, and I was so damn scared, remembering the horrific state of the remains of the wolves I saw. My eyes rolled in panic, and I could feel myself losing my grip on reality. My body shuddered, flashing first hot, then cold, a clammy sweat breaking out. I felt like a cornered, wounded animal. The air was not coming fast enough through my nostrils. The panic and fear was consuming me.

I'm gonna die, I'm gonna die, I'm gonna die.

Wait, something was happening...

I looked down at my body and saw my bones crack and break apart. My skin bubbled at the surface as the skeleton underneath tore apart. I screamed and screamed through the now-damp tape. Long, coarse red hair started sprouting from my pores.

The world dimmed as my eyes lost focus and turned blurry. Then, crystalline clarity appeared as my eyes slammed back into focus, sharper and clearer than before. My body hunched over as my spine reformed itself into an elongated curve.

I opened my widened mouth, the tape long gone. Out came a long tongue, panting and framed with a pair of sharp, knifelike fangs.

But the most startling change of all, I noticed a voice in my head, a sweet, pure consciousness besides my own.

What is holding us? We need to run; we need to be free! She whined.

My wolf!

My heart swelled with unbridled joy. I was finally whole! The other half of my soul finally merged as one.

I looked down and saw pure red fur, blazing and fiery like a flame. I threw back my head and howled to the rafters, shouting to the world my happiness. A happiness that was short-lived.

Suddenly, my head was slammed to the side, hitting the ground. My wolf whined out in confused pain. The human stood above us, that bat in his hand and a crazed grin on his face.

"I *knew* you were a wolf, you freak of nature, bitch!" He spat out gleefully, "I'm going to show you what your kind deserves."

He lifted the bat again and rained down blow after blow upon my wolf's delicate new body. I felt bones crunch as we howled in horror and pain.

Then everything went mercifully black again.

Chapter 10

Kayden

We raced back to the house, abandoning the pack business, after receiving Duncan's urgent text message he sent out to all of us repeatedly:

She's gone! Adrianna left! Come quick, I can't find her.

I burst into the front door and found Duncan pacing back and forth. He clutched at his hair and looked at me with guilty, panicked eyes.

"What did you do?!" I roared out. "Where is she?"

"She must've gotten the wrong idea! We were talking about babies and shit," he blurted out.

"And?" I said impatiently, not seeing the point.

"I must've scared her off or something. I thought she was taking a nap, but when I checked the room, she was gone," he replied frantically.

"And how long did it take you to pry yourself away from your precious books to check on our lovely omega?" I hissed at him with narrowed eyes.

He shifted his weight from foot to foot and opened his mouth. "I may have lost track of time while doing my research. But I had assumed..."

"So we already lost precious hours to track her down," I snapped, cutting him off.

"It's all my fault," Duncan muttered, shamefaced.

"None of us marked her, so we have no way of tracing her," I growled in frustration.

I lunged at Duncan, wrapping my hands around his neck. "How could you be so fucking stupid?"

"Hey, hey!" exclaimed Killian as he inserted himself between us, prying my hands off as best he could. But I was top alpha for a reason, and my hands didn't budge. Duncan was slowly turning purple, sputtering.

"Kayden, what the fuck? It could have been any of us," Killian tried to reach me desperately.

His words pierced through the haze of my rage, and I released my hands, letting Duncan drop to his knees, spluttering for a breath.

I roared out, releasing my anger to the walls. We finally had an omega, and we lost her. She was perfect in every way, and I got so fucking attached to her. We would find no one like her again. I knew that deep in my bones.

I slumped over to the couch, overwhelmed with sorrow.

Lucien wore a calculated look on his face, unlike the rest of us. The bastard had an idea. I was right when he opened his mouth.

"If she took the gray car, it would have had a tracker on it. Roman would never lend his cars unless there was a way for him to find it," he mused cunningly.

A flare of hope burst in my chest. I leaped up and clapped him on the back. "Good thinking, Lucien. Call Roman and have him send us the details."

We went back out and got into the large black SUV. We would need this space to punish our little naughty omega for running away. My cock hardened in anticipation of finding her, and I grinned.

After a few minutes, Lucien came back and wore a troubled expression on his face.

"According to Roman, the car has been sitting at a remote gas station for a while without moving," he stated.

Unease churned in my stomach at his words. Why would Adrianna stop so long in one place if she were trying to run away from us? She should've been putting miles between us.

"Could she have found out about the tracker and ditched the car?" Killian asked.

"That's impossible," Duncan rasped out, his throat an angry shade of red. "If we didn't even know about it, how could she?"

I ignored him. He had failed the pack, and I wasn't about to forgive him until we found our omega safe and sound. Regardless, we wouldn't find out anything until we got there. I got the location and started driving as fast as the car would allow, speeding through the roads with abandon.

We reached the gas station in a couple of hours, and I immediately spotted the gray car. It was the only vehicle in the tiny gas station. We walked up to it, and Adrianna was nowhere to be found. I sniffed the air. She was definitely here before.

Her caramel scent lingered in the air.

"Well, where the hell is she?" Killian blurted out, breaking the silence.

I scratched the back of my head. "I have no fucking clue." I was at a loss from here. I turned to Lucien, he was the best tracker among us. Sure enough, he didn't disappoint.

Lucien had kneeled on the ground in front of the driver's side of the car. He held up two red, glistening fingers and sniffed it.

"Blood," he stated coldly, "Adrianna's blood."

All our hackles were raised, and the station rumbled with our collective wolf's growls. This was so wrong. Her caramel-scented blood should never be spilled on this dirty pavement out here in the middle of nowhere.

"She didn't leave, she was taken," I said, numbly coming to that realization. Lucien nodded grimly, confirming my fears. Someone had dared to touch what wasn't theirs. They would die for this, painfully and slowly.

"I'm going to check the gas station surveillance to see if that shitty camera picked up on anything," Lucien said, springing into action. Duncan raced after him, desperate to redeem himself after his grievous mistake.

I tore off my clothes and shifted. This was going to be a fight to the death of whoever was foolish enough to kidnap our omega. My wolf was braying for blood, and I would not deny him. I paced around aggressively, stretching out my hind legs and shaking out my fur.

Besides me, Killian followed suit and shifted as well, howling to the night sky. We waited impatiently until Duncan and Lucien came running back, wearing identical grim looks on their faces. They ripped off their clothes and joined us in wolf form.

Lucien mind linked with us, showing images of a white van obscuring the view of Adrianna. Then he showed us images of the van leaving with Adrianna nowhere in sight.

And finally, a location of where the van was registered at. That was all the detail the poor-quality camera could show.

Beyond that, we had no idea what else had happened.

I howled to the moon and took off, pounding the earth with my paws. Behind me, I could hear my pack thundering away as well, and I grunted in approval. We were a force to be reckoned with, and whoever dared to take our omega was about to face the wrath of the Bloodmoon pack.

I sniffed around at an old, rusted gate. We had been running all night, stopping only for a brief water break. I did not feel fatigued in the least. My heart was pumping, knowing that we would soon rescue our mate.

The sun was rising, tendrils of light peeking through the cloudy sky. We had reached an old farm road that was barricaded by this flimsy gate.

I leaped over it, landing softly to not alert our enemy to our presence. One by one, the pack followed my lead, jumping over it with ease. I started up the dirt road, and then I smelled it.

Dried blood. Our mate's blood.

It was scattered in droplets up the pathway, but there was no mistaking that coppery scent. My eyes filmed over with a red haze from rage. Still, I padded softly up the pathway, hunting for my prey. The one who dared to spill her blood. The one who had signed their own death warrant.

And it was only one scent besides hers that I smelled. An old, pungent smell reminded me of rotting meat left out in the sun. It was not the clean scent of a wolf. A lone human had dared to do this.

I exchanged glances with Duncan, who was treading carefully beside me. I mind-linked with him, telling him to back off with the others.

The human was mine to kill.

Then, I saw him appear. The human. He exited from an old farmhouse, swinging something by his side. He did not look around at his surroundings but focused intently on an old barn, making his way towards that. A shame. Maybe if he had looked around, he might've seen his impending doom. Instead, he trudged along his path, oblivious to the predator hunting him.

I came up softly behind him and saw with bone-chilling horror what he was swinging so casually by his side.

It was a baseball bat... coated with my mate's precious caramel-scented blood. My mind fucking snapped. I let my animal instincts fully take over. There was going to be no slow, torturous end for this human. My wolf demanded his death now.

I leaped over his hand, landing right in front of him, baring my fangs with a deafening growl. I needed to see his face as he died. I allowed him one moment of pure shock.

"Wha...," he started to gasp out. He never got to finish what he wanted to say.

My claws shot out and ripped open his belly, spilling out his intestines to the dirt ground below. He dropped to his knees, his face graying with his eyes rolling to the back of his head. He spluttered, his worthless blood pouring out of his mouth.

I leaped onto his chest, knocking him fully to the ground. I opened my mouth, baring my fangs, and ripped out his neck with a satisfying crunch. I let his decapitated head drop unceremoniously, letting it roll to a stop on the blood-soaked earth. My pack gathered around, howling in victory and ripping apart his disgusting body.

But our hunt was not over yet. We still needed to find Adrianna and bring her back to her rightful place with her pack.

Chapter 11

Kayden

I raced to the wooden barn door the human was heading towards, still in my wolf form. It was locked, secured with a chain and padlock. The scent of blood was stronger here. I had no key. I growled for a second, deciding what to do.

Without further ado, I threw my heavy wolf's body against it over and over. I heard creaking, the wooden door splintering, embedding itself into my fur. Uncaring about the pain, I threw myself against it harder. Blood poured down my shoulders, dripping hot.

The pack joined me, using our collective strength.

Finally, it gave way with a deafening crash, falling into the room ahead. Cheerful sunlight poured into the room, illuminating the horror within. My blood ran cold.

Our beautiful, red-furred Adrianna in wolf form, broken, bloodied, and chained to the wall. All I could see were the giant manacles around each of her four limbs and her limpness as she lay there unmoving. My wolf let out a last pained roar, letting me take over now. He knew the chains were not something his claws could manage.

I shifted to my human form, uncaring of my nakedness. I raced over to her and felt her pulse. It was faint but there. My body shuddered as I beheld the torture that had been rained down upon her.

My eyes could not see a single bone that had not been broken or a piece of fur that had not been bloodied. If she were in her human form, she would have died ages ago. Her wolf had kept her alive.

Murderous rage overwhelmed my rational thought. I wanted to go back and kill that evil, vile pig all over again.

Instead, I grasped the first manacle around her front paw with my bare hands. I braced myself, muscles bulging.

The rusted metal cut into my hands as I tore it apart with a vicious strength I didn't know I possessed.

I tossed the broken cuffs aside and reached for the second. Blood poured down my arms as I shattered the second one as well. The metal had cut through my nerves and tendons until it had reached the white bone of my hands.

Despite that, I reached for the third manacle.

My shredded hands were shaking with pure agony as it slipped from my grasp. I reached for it again, intent on destroying the thing keeping me from my mate. But my ravaged hands could not grasp it.

Then Duncan appeared there, in his human form as well. He held an ax in his hand.

"I got this. Just steady her leg for me," he said grimly.

I grasped her red-furred limb and braced it the best I could. I could no longer feel the use of my hands. Duncan carefully lined up the ax and brought it down with a shattering force. The cuff instantly broke into shards.

The force of the hit vibrated up my arms, sending shooting waves of paralyzing pain through my destroyed hands. Blackness tinged at my vision, but I fought it. I would see our mate to safety, no matter the cost to myself.

Finally, the last cuff was broken off of her. Waves of nausea rolled through me at the intense pain, but I shrugged it off and gathered her up in my arms, careful not to jostle her and cause further damage.

I barked at Lucien, who was standing guard at the door in his human form.

"Find a car, any car! She is in no shape to travel on foot."

His eyes widened, and his face paled at the state of Adrianna in my bloodied arms. If he was shocked, it was bad. Without a word, he turned on his heel and ran back towards the farmhouse. In my mindless hunt for her, I only thought about reaching her as quickly as possible. I cursed myself a thousand different ways for not thinking this far ahead. I should've brought a healer along as well.

We would have to travel back to our hometown. The Bloodmoon Pack had the best healers alongside the best fighters in the country. I turned back towards Duncan.

"Get a phone and send word for the jet to meet us at the nearest airport!"

He took off after Lucien, leaving a trail of dust and blood in his wake.

I cradled Adrianna close to my chest. I pleaded with the universe.

Please, please let her make it out alive.

I would let no other harm come to her again. I would protect our mate with my mind, body, and soul to my dying day. She just needed to get through this alive.

"Hurry up!" I roared out.

Lucien pulled up in an old, white van, the tires squealing as he slammed the brakes to a stop in front of me. Killian opened the van door, and I carefully climbed in, carrying my precious load.

I settled Adrianna carefully onto my lap. She let out a shallow breath. Her wolf was petite and slender, with a beautiful long tail. Her fiery red tail was the only part of her untouched by horror. She fit perfectly in my arms.

Duncan dove into the passenger seat beside Lucian.

"I called ahead using the house's landline. The jet will land at the airport in thirty minutes. We have a forty-minute drive, clear of traffic," said Duncan.

I nodded at him stiffly. We still weren't moving fast enough to my liking. I caught sight of Killian standing in front of the barn. He threw a lighter into the open barn door, and flames immediately shot out. He jumped into the van beside me seconds later, and we peeled off.

The remains of the other werewolves tortured inside that barn did not escape my notice. The human deserved to die repeatedly for what he did. While not a formal werewolf burial, a cremation would hopefully put the haunted souls to rest at least. A solemn silence fell over the van as we started our race to the airport.

I breathed in Adrianna's scent, intoxicated by the sweet perfume of it, present under all the layers of blood and dirt. My wolf's hearing kept careful track of her heartbeat, noticing how it slowed more and more as time passed.

"Drive faster, dammit!" I snapped at Lucien. His icy face remained expressionless as he pushed the accelerator to its limits, the van's hinges squeaking with the strain.

Then, I felt a twitch in my arms. Adrianna was trying to wake up, to shift back. *But that could kill her.*

"No, Adrianna, darling! You can't shift back just yet. Hold on, my love."

Her wolf's eyes opened and rolled with panic as she took in her surroundings. Her breath came in heaves, and I heard her heartbeat picking up at an incredibly fast pace. A dangerously fast pace I knew her heart could not sustain for long.

"Don't let her shift back," said Duncan worriedly.

She jerked in my arms, trying to break free, reopening her wounds and bleeding freely all over the van seats. Her wolf whined and whimpered in heartbreaking terror. I held her down as best I could without further injuring her.

"Adrianna! Baby, calm down! You're going to be okay!" I desperately tried to reach her.

Eventually, her wolf passed out again and lay limp in my arms once more. The van came to a swift stop. We reached the airport tarmac right as the jet touched down in front of us. Lucian couldn't have timed it better.

Duncan jumped out and slammed the van door open. We raced to the jet and got in. Her slowing heartbeat echoed in my ears. I glanced over at all the gray faces sitting around me. Everyone wore lines of exhaustion and fatigue after our long run.

"What's the ETA?" I asked Duncan.

"Two hours, and that's pushing it to the limit," he replied grimly.

I fought off the waves of hopelessness. She would live goddammit.

"She's going to make it, she's going to make it," I chanted to myself, hopefully projecting that into her mind and spirit even if unconscious.

I held her for the duration of the flight, allowing no one else to help me. My hands felt like wooden stumps on the ends of my arms, completely useless. At least they stopped bleeding freely, and the pain numbed out a while ago.

Finally, after what felt like an eternity, we landed. I shot up from my seat, using the last bit of adrenaline left that I had.

Lucian slammed the emergency door open, rolled out the stairs, and leaped out of my way. I pounded down the stairs, careful to keep my balance and not shift Adrianna any more than necessary.

Finally, the goddamn healers! *Thank fucking god!*

I've never been happier to see the black-robed, elderly healers of the Bloodmoon pack in all my life. They were there waiting with a gurney already set up and a nearby tent erected.

They had clearly been warned ahead of time of the gravity of the situation. Their alpha wolves' new mate hovered between life and death. The fate of the future of their pack lay in their hands. They took her from my arms, and I was left suddenly empty and bereft like a boat without a sail.

An elderly healer approached me tentatively.

"Alpha Kayden, allow me to see to your hands," she rasped out.

"No! Save Adrianna with the rest of them."

She harrumphed, not used to being spoken sharply towards at her advanced age. But she pivoted on her heel, her agility defying her age, and followed her fellow healers to the now bustling tent.

We had completed our purpose. We rescued our mate and slain her enemies. She was brought to the healers. Now, we were helpless in the face of destiny. Strength, speed, and endurance had no place now. I exchanged solemn glances with Duncan, Lucien, and Killian.

What the hell could we do now?

Chapter 12

Adrianna

I was lost between worlds.

I drifted through states of consciousness and unconsciousness, through blinding pain and numbing bliss. I saw flashes of the human man evilly grinning, whose face turned into Kayden's compassion-filled gaze. The van, the horrid van, I was back in it.

Images blurred together in a confusing haze.

No! I had to escape. I fought weakly but drifted off again into the unknown. The sensation of weightlessness. Being surrounded by warm male presences. Multiple males lending strength, love, and peace.

Then, I faded again into the blackness.

I woke up to the sound of birds chirping and felt sunlight warming my face. I was too afraid to open my eyes, terrified of what I was going to see next. I bravely peeked one eye open and gasped in shock.

I was in a beautiful, golden room, lying in a soft, fluffy cloud of bedding. I was in the middle of a giant, majestic bed in the center of the most luxurious room I had ever seen.

Did I die and make it to heaven?

The golden, intricate door eased open, and Killian slowly walked in, holding a washcloth in his hand. My heart jumped at the sight. Oh god, how I had missed him! A warm, familiar face.

He didn't notice I was awake. His face was crestfallen as he carefully made his way to the bed.

"Killian," I rasped out, my throat feeling sore and scratchy.

His head snapped up, and his gaze met mine.

"Adrianna! You're awake! Oh my god!"

He raced over to me and gingerly sat next to me, showering my face with kisses. I giggled and tried to bat him away and realized my hands and arms were covered in thick, tightly wrapped bandages.

Then I remembered what happened and sobered up.

"How did you find me?" I whispered to him. Tears blurred my vision as I remembered the horror I had endured.

"Lucien tracked you, darling. It was a hell of a hunt, but we found you in the end," he said grimly, stroking my hair.

Lucien walked in right at that moment. His eyes widened, seeing that I was awake, and he broke into a smile, the first I had ever seen on him. I let the tears flow freely down my cheeks, and the gratitude shine through my eyes.

"Thank you, Lucien, for finding me. I would have been dead if it weren't for you," I choked out, overcome with emotion.

"Ah, little omega, I'll always be there to find you," he said, his face turning red.

He sat on the other side of me and placed my hand carefully on his lap. I felt rumbling vibrations emanating from them both, and peace washed over me. I closed my eyes and hummed in response.

"What are you guys doing?" I gasped out. My throat felt considerably less swollen.

"Our alpha energy can help you heal a little faster," explained Lucien. "If we were bonded, you probably would have been healed already," he admonished lightly.

I bit my lip and looked away. I still remembered why I had run away in the first place. But all that seemed trivial in the face of what had just happened. This pack was there for me when no one else was, and I would never forget that.

Duncan walked into the room, and waves of guilt rolled over me about how I tricked him and took advantage of his kind, trusting nature. He came to a stop at the door of the bed and looked me over.

"I'm glad you're looking a lot better now, love," he said gently.

"I'm sorry, Duncan," I blurted out. "I.."

He shushed me before I could continue, sitting right at my feet.

"The past is the past, love. I just want you to focus on healing now."

I nodded, my heart swelling with love for this gracious and sweet alpha. I closed my eyes, intending to rest for a while, but the door opened once more, letting in the final alpha of my pack.

I opened my eyes and gulped nervously. Kayden stood there in all his glory. But unlike the others, he wore a mask of indifference and kept his arms clasped behind his back.

"Kayden," I squeaked out tentatively, breaking the silence.

"After you're all healed up, we'll return you to the official omega nest, where you can await a pack of your own choosing," he stated formally.

I gasped in hurt pain, and it wasn't from my wounds.

"Perhaps you will be lucky and find another pack to go into heat with. Good luck with your future," he finished up his speech, turned on his heel, and left the room.

"You guys are giving me up?" I cried out, scanning the rest of their saddened faces.

"Isn't that what you had wanted?" Killian replied bleakly.

"You didn't want us, remember?" Lucien added.

"Well, I changed my mind. I just needed some time to think," I said, wearing my heart on my sleeve. "Obviously, I don't want any babies right now..." my voice trailed off as I yawned.

Duncan jumped in, interfering. "Look, guys, this conversation can wait for another time. Right now, you need rest. As much as you can get, love."

His words warmed my heart, and I nodded obediently, resting my head back and closing my eyes, surrounded by my rumbling alphas. Only for the time being, I thought sadly.

For the next few days, I slept and ate. Slowly, I was regaining my strength and healing rapidly, thanks to the energies emitting from my alphas. I always had two alphas on either side of me at all times. I admit, it was great to actually get to know them on a personal level.

Killian was the most fun to hang out with. He regaled me with crazy adventure stories and made me laugh till my sides ached. Duncan made me feel safe and loved, and we had deep conversations on many topics. Lucien was a little hard to get to know at first, and he mostly steered the conversations towards me and what I liked.

But the worst alpha to hang out with was Kayden. I found out he had suffered the most damage on the hunt to save me, and I wondered if he was holding a grudge or something. Our sessions were spent in stony silence or sleep.

There was no conversation forthcoming from him.

And honestly, I didn't even care at this point. I had too much pride to beg him to keep me. If he didn't want to have me in his pack, then I would be more than happy to walk away with my freedom. But the thought of leaving tore my heart to pieces.

I had already seen the bleak world outside, and I had no more interest in going out there.

My family was here now, and I knew deep in my heart that I would be happy here. But Kayden never brought up the subject again, and I refused to talk about it as well. I guess when the day came when I was fully healed, we would see what would happen.

Killian

I threw down the matching Uno card I had in my hand and waited for Adrianna's turn. She had taken a liking to this card game, and we played it almost nonstop during our sessions now.

But it killed me to see Adrianna sad like this. She tried to hide it during our session by laughing at my lame jokes, but I could see the pain in her eyes. She clearly said she didn't want to leave our pack anymore, but asshole Kayden wouldn't budge on the issue.

He claims he wants to give her a proper choice for her future after the ordeal that had happened to her. Truth be told, I think he's blaming himself for what happened. For taking away her choice and "forcing" her to take such drastic action that almost cost her life.

Regardless, all I knew was that I wanted to keep this fiery redhead as our omega. But Kayden wouldn't give in and I could see Adrianna would never ask him. So we all tiptoed around that topic, never actually discussing it.

"Uno, again!" Adrianna exclaimed, throwing her hands up with glee.

She was healing faster by the day and was almost fully better. She still stayed in bed, however, as that was the easiest way to surround her. Duncan was on shift with me, his nose buried in a book on Adrianna's right side.

"Ah, you win again, darling," I drawled out.

I leaned forward and captured her plump pink lips in a deep kiss. She pulled away, flustered, her cheeks turning red.

"We can't do that sort of stuff. I'm still healing," she stated, unsure of her own words.

Duncan raised a brow but continued flipping through his book silently. Good man.

"You know, being closer to you like this will help you heal even faster, darling," I said, running a finger over her visible cleavage.

She shivered and stared at me with widened eyes. "But we're not even a pack anymore," she protested weakly.

"That's not fair now, is it?" I said seductively. "You allowed the others to knot you, but not me, remember?"

Her cheeks flushed even further, and she turned away. "My heat was over pretty quick," she admitted, acknowledging my claim.

I groaned and kissed her mouth again, lingering with my tongue. I broke the kiss and backed off, a twinkle in my eye. She wasn't healed enough yet for what I wanted to do with her. But she damn well will be in horny anticipation for it.

"Big mistake, darling. Now I'm gonna have to show you what you missed out on." I teased her.

She laughed at my threat, but I could smell her slick from here. I was turning her on.

I forced myself to get up and leave the room, to get myself back under control. But soon, regardless of what Kayden says, that sexy omega would have my knot buried deep inside her right where it belonged.

Chapter 13

Kayden

Adrianna was insisting on taking a bath today. It was my session time with her and she absolutely refused to wait a second longer "without soaking in bubbles".

"Look, Kayden, I'll either do this with your help or without it. But just so you know, if I hurt myself, it's on you," she said bossily, her nose high in the air.

I wanted to uncross her arms and pin them up on the wall above her while I entered her slowly. Then she would see who was the boss...

I shook my head, eliminating that particular train of thought. *She wasn't our omega anymore.*

"Fine, let's just get this over with," I grumbled.

I reluctantly helped her out of bed and walked her slowly to the bathroom. She was still a little shaky on her feet, but nothing too serious, thankfully. I sat her down on the closed toilet and turned to the bath to fill it up.

I saw movement from the corner of my eye. Was she taking off that long, hideous nightgown the healers had forced her into? The thought of her slowly revealing her luscious body made my cock spring to life in my pants.

I clenched my teeth and focused on adding an acceptable amount of bubbly soap to the rising bathwater. I didn't dare look behind me to see what she was doing or I knew my control would snap.

I turned off the water once the bath was full and averted my gaze. "You can go in now," I said gruffly.

She didn't move.

"Well?" I inquired. "Why aren't you going in?"

"I'm... afraid I might fall. I don't think I can lift my leg over the edge by myself," she said sweetly.

Fucking hell.

"Fine," I said, letting the irritation show in my tone. I braced myself before turning, but even that wasn't enough to help get over the stunning sight of her toned, naked body. Most of her bruises and cuts were healed, except for a large portion of her right leg.

Other than that, her skin gleamed with health and vitality. Her breasts were perfection with pebbled, pink tips that were just begging to be sucked. Her thatch of blazing red hair covered her pussy from my sight.

Her eyes danced with amusement as she watched me take in the sight of her body.

I quickly snapped back my mask of indifference and I held out an arm for her to grab onto. *If only she would grab onto something a little lower...*

But no.

She would have rather died than be mated to us, and I learned my lesson. I would never force her to be mated to us, and I vowed to give her a choice in determining her own future. She did not acknowledge any desire to stay with this pack, and so I would proceed with my plan to return her.

Even though it hurt my chest so much, it was hard to breathe.

She gingerly stepped one foot up and over into the bath and stood there, legs splayed wide open. One foot in and one foot out. With her legs open, her pussy lips were exposed and I could smell her caramel scent more strongly, mixed in with the scent of slick.

Her slick.

I longed to kneel between her conveniently placed legs and swipe my tongue from the top of her clit to her asshole. Over and over again

"Is there a problem?" I grunted out between clenched teeth.

"I don't have the strength to lift my other leg over," she said in that extra sugary voice. "I think I'm stuck," she continued, batting her lashes up at me. She wiggled her bottom to emphasize her point. Her tanned orbs jiggled right where I could see them.

Ah... she was playing me. Well, two could play that game.

I cupped her pussy with one hand, barely brushing her slick covered clit with my index finger.

She gasped at my touch. I placed my other hand on her lower back and gently lifted her up and into the bath. I left my hand on her pussy and let my fingers twitch ever so slightly over her clit, sending shockwaves of sensation through her body.

I slowly pulled my hand away, letting it drag through her slick.

"There you go, baby," I said roughly, as affected by the encounter as she was.

I backed up, and she blinked up at me in shock. She was expecting me to go further, but I wouldn't. Not unless she acknowledged us as her mated pack for life. Until then, she would not get any fingers, knots or cocks anywhere near her and definitely not in her.

She glared at me, all the sugariness gone from her posture, and sat down in her bath, facing away from me. She realized I caught on to her little game and was pouting.

I grinned.

This was going to be fun. She roughly started scrubbing herself, and I laughed outright.

"Do you mind keeping it down? I'm trying to relax," she snapped at me, looking over her bare shoulder.

That only made me laugh harder. "Go ahead, baby, you go on and relax."

"You're right, I should relax."

A sly look came over her face and she turned fully in the bath to face me. She propped her good leg over the edge and wiggled one finger at me. She stuck it in her mouth, swirling and sucking it thoroughly.

Fuck.

My balls tightened up and my dick was rock hard. I could almost imagine it was my dick and her mouth and she was swirling her tongue all over it.

She released her finger from her mouth with a loud smacking pop. Then she trailed that finger down her neck and circled each breast. Then she went further down her stomach, where it disappeared into the water. By the way she threw her head back and moaned, it was pretty obvious where her finger had gone.

I pulled my cock out of my pants and started pulling on it. If only the water wasn't so damn bubbly, then I could see exactly what her finger was doing. Was she furiously rubbing the clit I had just brushed on moments ago? Or was she thrusting that tiny finger into her hungry pussy that was craving a large knot to fill it up?

"Tell me what you're doing, baby," I rumbled to her, beating my cock harder. Drops of pre-cum seeped out of the head of it.

"I'm relaxing, Kayden, just like you said," she replied, oh so innocently.

Her hand was moving furiously under the water and her cheeks were flushed pink. Her breath came out in gasps and she quickened her rhythm.

She threw her back and her body jerked as her orgasm hit her hard. Her eyes fluttered shut, and she let out a long, throaty moan.

I couldn't hold out any longer and my cum shot out in thick streams all over the bathroom floor. She looked at my cock and licked her full lips. *Fuck*. My dick twitched one more time, releasing a final spurt of cum.

I couldn't stay for any more of her games. I don't know how long I could hold out before I gave in to all her teasing and fucked her just the way she needed me to. I had to wait until she agreed to be a part of our pack. Until then, I needed to keep my distance.

"Killian will help you finish up your bath," I said, cleaning myself and leaving.

I saw a flash of disappointment in her eyes before I turned away. Why did she want me to fuck her, anyway? Did she want one more fling before she set off to find herself a new pack, or was she simply horny?

I shook my head in confusion as I headed out and alerted Killian to his session with her.

Adrianna

I splashed at the water angrily. Wasn't an omega basically a drug for an alpha? Why was it so hard for me to seduce Kayden?

I probably was a defective omega, I thought with a sigh.

At least I had my wolf now. I could feel her presence in the back of mind at all times. Duncan had told me omegas rarely shift since it uses up so much energy. Supposedly, most of my energy went towards producing slick and enhancing my natural scent to attract alphas.

Something that didn't seem to work on Kayden, I thought in frustration.

If I could get him to mate with and mark me through his own choice, then maybe he wouldn't give me away to the omega nest. I was so close to opening my mouth and begging him for his thick knot, but I just couldn't surrender to him like that.

The modern college girl part of me absolutely detested the thought of submitting to him in that way.

So until then, I gritted my teeth in pent up horniness. My finger was not enough to satisfy my needs and my ploys to get his knot failed.

Killian walked in, breaking my train of thought. He whistled at the sight of me and made himself comfortable.

I blushed furiously. Out of all the alphas, I felt the most shy when I was with him. Maybe it was because he was the only one left who hadn't knotted me, or it was because he always had a crazed gleam in his eye.

He had an untamed, wild side that scared and excited me at the same time. Either way, I knew I was playing with fire when I was with him.

I turned to reach over for some much needed shampoo. Weeks of bed rest were not a good look on my hair.

"You know, I can help you with that," drawled out Killian.

I raised an eyebrow. I didn't believe for a second that he didn't have some ulterior motive.

"Okay, thanks," I slowly replied, handing the shampoo bottle to him anyway. Maintaining my long hair wasn't easy, and I was glad for the help. My arms still felt a bit sore.

To my surprise, he got up and started stripping off his clothes.

"What are you doing?!" I spluttered out.

"Helping you wash your hair, darling," he replied innocently, pulling down his pants and letting his long cock spring free.

Chapter 14

Killian

I got into the large warm bath and positioned myself behind Adrianna, placing her between my splayed legs.

True to my word, I picked up the shampoo bottle and started lathering up her rich, red locks. I massaged her scalp thoroughly and then moved down to her shoulder blades and back.

"Oh, this feels so freakin' good," she moaned out with her eyes closed.

My dick moved against her back and she didn't pull away. I slowly slid my hands to her front and held her big tits in my hands, squeezing and kneading them.

She rested her head back against my chest and allowed me to play with her slippery breasts. I pinched and pulled at her nipples, watching her breath quickening at my touch. She spread her legs wide and mewled in frustration, thrusting up into the empty air.

I chuckled.

"Are you desperate for my cock, darling?"

"Yes," she gasped out. *Oh fuck!*

There wasn't any more time for games. I turned her around and made her straddle my lap. I wanted to see her lovely green eyes as I sank into her pussy for the first time. I lined up my cock at her entrance and dragged her down onto my long length.

Most women couldn't handle the full length of my cock, so I stopped just a few inches shy of fully putting it in. I reached down between us and strummed at her clit. She moved her hips and unabashedly rode me, taking her pleasure.

She held her own tits in her hands and played with herself, bouncing up and down. Then she sank down fully onto me, my dick bottoming out inside her. My eyes widened as I felt her pussy envelop my dick fully and completely. I froze in shock as she continued riding me without missing a beat.

"Darling, am I hurting you?" I asked her urgently.

She laughed and threw her head back.

"Of course not, I needed this so bad!"

I should've known my fated omega could handle my cock. It was meant for her, after all.

I grinned and gripped her hips, loving the feeling of fully slapping into her pussy. For the first time, I could feel a woman's clit grinding against my lower navel and I held her there, deep inside. I rubbed circles against her clit as I stayed buried as deep as I possibly could.

The grip of her pussy was out of this world, spasming all around my cock.

Adrianna

I needed this so fucking bad. After my failed attempt at seducing Kayden, having Killian's cock buried so deep inside of me was exactly what I had needed. I rode up and down, loving his long length that hit me in all the right places.

My orgasm took me by surprise and I screamed it out, just as Lucien walked in and made eye contact with me. That made my orgasm last even longer.

"Well, well, well, look who's breaking the rules," he smirked.

He didn't wait for a reply before tearing off his shirt and pants in a split second and joining us in the tub.

Killian didn't pause in his lovemaking and continued to thrust into me. My pussy lips felt achy and swollen, desperate for his knot, but he wasn't done anytime soon. Suddenly, I felt a finger teasing the entrance of my butt.

Lucien was sitting at my back, the large tub easily accommodating all of us. He used his finger to play with my butthole, stroking the outside and stretching my entrance.

"Is this okay, little omega?" he asked me, right by my ear.

"I think so," I breathed out. It didn't hurt, so it must be okay. He inserted two fingers and stretched me even further. I felt slick seeping out from that hole and mixing in with the bath water.

"Fuck, little omega, your tight hole is more than ready for my cock," he groaned out. Then his hand disappeared and in its place was a thick cock, pushing its head through my entrance.

Killian paused on bouncing me up and down his cock, so that Lucien could ease his way inside my untouched ass. Lucien grabbed each of my buttcheeks and spread them wide, to facilitate his dick. His thick head slowly made its way in, stretching my puckered skin.

I felt so full, unsure if I was able to take in anymore. Killian, feeling me tense up, started rubbing my clit again to help me relax.

"Relax, darling, you got this," he murmured to me.

Inch by inch, I took in Lucien's cock alongside Killian's. Finally, he was seated in all the way. Then the magic happened.

When Killian would thrust out, Lucien would thrust in. They established an alternating rhythm, so my body was never without an alpha cock. I screamed out my pleasure, sandwiched between these two large alphas.

Suddenly, they changed their pace. Instead of alternating, they both thrust into me at the same time. I gasped at the fullness of it. My pussy and asshole were stretched out so wide. My clit was still being rubbed. In my haze of pleasure, I couldn't tell who was rubbing it.

Another orgasm hit me hard, and my voice was hoarse from screaming. My pussy clenched helplessly around Killian's cock, and my ass gripped Lucien's firmly. They continued bouncing me through my orgasm until I melted bonelessly between them.

Killian came with a shout spurting deep inside me, and his knot immediately swelled up. Lucien hastened his pace and reached his climax as well, before Killian's knot made it too difficult to continue. His knot swelled up as well. And then I was locked in between both of them, stuffed full of Alpha knots.

The busy bathroom door opened up once again. This time it was Kayden, probably coming back to argue some more.

He stopped dead in his tracks and his eyes widened at the sight of me full of alpha knots.

"What the hell is going on in here?!" He exclaimed to Killian and Lucien. Outrage was written all over his face. "I told you guys not to touch her!"

I interfered before they could reply. "I am fucking my pack, as is my right. What the hell are *you* doing in here?" I said haughtily, turning the tables on him.

He stood there dumbfounded for a few moments. Then a slow grin spread out across his face. "Your pack, eh?" He repeated back to me.

"That's right, *my* pack," I emphasized my point by leaning forward and kissing Killian's mouth, tongue and all.

"Duncan! Get in here! It seems our omega needs one more knot in her mouth." Kayden called out the door.

Duncan came bursting in, hope flaring in his eyes. "Does this mean we get to keep her?"

"She seems to have claimed us, so yes, we will keep our omega," Kayden announced to the room at large.

My heart sang at his words, but I was careful to keep the emotion off of my face so I don't inflate his already too big ego. I kept my haughty indifference mask on my face, taking a page from Lucien's book.

Duncan approached us and removed his pants. He didn't even bother removing his shirt before sitting on the edge of the tub. His thick cock was inches away from my mouth.

"Can you handle one more knot, love?" He asked me gently.

I didn't even reply, instead I eagerly reached over and placed the ruddy head inside my mouth. I didn't have any practice at giving blowjobs, but from what other girls had said, the head was supposed to be the most sensitive.

I focused my attentions on the wide mushroomed tip, swirling and sucking away. I ran my tongue over the ridge underneath the head and he gasped and jerked into my mouth. The room was filled with the sound of me slurping on dick.

Duncan tensed up and shot his load into my mouth. I let his cum drip down to my chin and maintained eye contact with him as his knot started swelling up. I kept it in my mouth, wanting to feel the sensation of three full knots in me. I breathed out carefully through my nose as his thick knot filled my mouth.

Kayden stood over us all, a satisfied gleam in his eye as he took in his pack knotting their omega.

Killian's knot released me first, followed quickly by Lucien's. They pulled out of me carefully, and I let go of Duncan's knot in my mouth. I looked around at the bath water and felt slightly grossed out.

I had really wanted a nice hot bath to wash away my ordeal.

"Everybody, out please. I need to take a proper shower and wash away germs and whatnot," I commanded out.

I really loved my authoritative voice. I should use it more often.

Lucien lifted me up onto the tub edge to sit on, while Killian drained the tub for me.

Kayden spoke up while we were waiting. "Adrianna, I'd like to show you a proper tour of our home tomorrow if you're feeling up to it."

"Yes! I'm getting sick of staring at the same four walls. It's finally time to leave my room." I said excitedly.

Apparently, they had flown me out to the official Bloodmoon pack lands while I was in critical condition. I had been on bed rest since I had arrived and I had no idea what the rest of the house or lands looked like.

While this bathtub experience was a pleasurable distraction, I really wanted to see the outside world and get a chance to breathe some fresh air.

I happily got into the freshly scrubbed shower that Killian had prepared for me. I waved goodbye to my pack before closing the shower curtain and scrubbing away all the germs I was imagining in my head.

I felt on top of the world with happiness. Kayden was not going to give me away to the omega nest. My body had healed faster than I thought possible. And, most of all, I had a wonderful, amazing pack that would go through hell and back to make sure that I was safe.

I relaxed into the hot spray of the shower and wondered how I had gotten so lucky. After running away from Kayden and his pack, I could see how cruel and ugly the world could be. My parents had shielded me from the worst of it, especially by hiding my omega nature. But now I knew, as an omega, I could never live on my own and I needed a pack to survive.

Kayden and his alphas were my future, and I was ready to see the Bloodmoon pack lands and accept it as my new home.

Chapter 15

Kayden

Everything needed to be perfect for when Adrianna toured the grounds. Our pack was much larger than most, and we functioned as a sort of little village. There was the main house, where me and the other alphas lived. And now Adrianna. My mouth curled up in a grin. She had boldly claimed her pack yesterday and decided to stay with us after all.

Surrounding the main house were tiny shops that the numerous betas living in my lands ran. They all lived in a large apartment complex right next to a beautiful lake.

They sometimes frequented the human stores for specific supplies or services if the beta stores did not have it.

Everything was well organized, maintained and ran smoothly.

I headed back to the house, a little nervous to see Adrianna's reaction to it all. What if she hated it and demanded to return to her home? What if she changed her mind about wanting to be with this pack?

I shoved those feelings way deep down inside and made my way to her room.

My breath caught in my throat as I beheld the gorgeous omega. She sat at the dressing table, brushing out her long, wavy red hair. It glinted, reflecting out the sunlight. She wore an emerald green dress that hugged her curves in all the right places and a dramatic smokey eye look.

She turned to me and smiled, and I had to restrain myself from going over there and rutting into her like a beast.

Today was going to be perfect, I reminded myself. We were going to show her the grounds and take her out on a proper date. The goal was to charm her, not fuck her. I willed my erection to stay down and not be so obvious in my pants.

"Are you ready for your tour, gorgeous?" I said, making my way over to her.

"Yes," she said. " I just don't have a pair of shoes on me. I've been in bed all these days."

"I got you, baby," Duncan walked in carrying a brand new shoe box.

I glared at him as he walked by. I wanted to be the one to provide for her today, and I didn't like him interfering. He smirked at me as she opened the box and exclaimed over the shoes. They were glittery green flats that matched her dress and her eyes perfectly.

Killian walked in next, wearing a suit and holding a bouquet of flowers. I gaped at him. Never in my life have I seen him wearing a suit. This was clearly a sabotage.

They didn't tell me we were bringing gifts.

I felt foolish standing there with nothing as she gushed over the smell of the "perfectly picked" roses. I glared at Killian, and he shrugged. At least I knew Lucien wouldn't stoop down to their level. I prepared my arm to escort the lovely Adrianna, but she gasped, looking past my shoulder.

I closed my eyes.

I didn't even want to see the romantic monstrosity that Lucien had come up with. His depraved mind wasn't capable of sweet and happy thoughts. I heard Duncan and Killian letting out muffled snickers that turned into outright laughter.

I braced myself and turned around and let out my own snort of laughter.

Lucien stood there with a huge pink basket in his arms. The content of the basket was empty and instead was hopped up on his shoulder. A fluffy white rabbit with long floppy ears that was currently shitting on his shirt.

"Omegas are said to enjoy the company of bunnies," he explained through clenched teeth, a pained look on his face.

"That is so sweet, Lucien," said Adrianna, rushing over to hug the bunny. "You guys stop laughing at him. I love it so much!" She exclaimed, peppering Lucien's face with kisses.

"So sweet, Lucien," Killian repeated with a straight face.

"Yes, so sweet," Duncan added, guffawing loudly.

Lucien's face turned bright red, and he turned on his heel, muttering something about changing his shirt and don't wait up for him.

Adrianna admonished us, and she hugged and cuddled the bunny close to her chest. My cock hardened even more watching her stroke and sweet-talked the lucky bastard.

I bet every alpha in the room wished they were that bunny right at this moment.

Adrianna

After much coaxing, I placed the adorable bunny down in the pink basket.

He was so cuddly and his scent made me want to stay in and play with him all day long. Lucien was right. I was super attached to the bunny the minute I laid eyes on him. Kayden had to assure me multiple times that someone would check up on him while we were out and about.

I put on the super cute flats and smelled the flowers one last time before heading out of the room on Kayden's arm. Excitement fluttered in my belly and I couldn't wait for the tour to start.

First, we toured the place we were staying and my jaw dropped. The mansion we had stayed at in West Virginia was a child's dollhouse compared to where we were now. This felt more like a palace, complete with butlers, maids, chefs, gardeners, security guards and whatnot.

Everything was gilded and golden, and it literally felt like I had stepped into heaven.

I oohed and ahhed in every room, and Kayden's chest swelled up in satisfaction and pride. I could tell he was a little nervous showing me his home and my reactions were completely genuine. It was a magnificent home, and it felt like we were royalty.

We exited the house and walked out onto the perfectly manicured grounds. I saw children squealing and running freely, playing games on the lawn, and my heart melted. In the far distance, I could see a cute little ice cream shop.

"Oh my god! We are so going there!" I squealed out.

"Anything for you, baby," Kayden said sweetly, and my heart melted even further.

He called over a golf cart and helped me up inside. He walked over to the driver's spot and sat in. The others piled in behind us. They were letting him take the lead on this outing. I sat down, grateful for the rest. Truth be told, my legs were getting a little sore touring the entire palace like home.

It was a hell of a lot of walking, and I knew I couldn't make it all the way to the ice cream shop on my own.

I sat back; the wind flew through my hair as we made our way over to the shop. Killian made his usual jokes while Duncan brought up the current news. Lucien remained silent as was his norm and Kayden pointed out various buildings that we passed by.

We reached the ice cream shop and walked in. The beta owner hurried over to welcome us in, honored to have the alphas of the pack in his store.

"Over here we have our newly renovated, private omega room, so you can all be more comfortable." He said, showing us up the stairs, past the regular customer tables.

We went into the opulent room, and it was full of pink fur and various seating pillows with a low, round table in the middle. He gave us the ice cream menu and closed the door, telling us to call him when we were ready for our orders.

"Omega room? Were you guys mated before to another omega?" I said, unexpected pangs of jealousy shooting through me at the thought of them enjoying this room with another omega.

Kayden laughed and hugged me close.

"No, baby. I open my pack lands and allow other packs to visit here, and sometimes their alphas bring their omegas along with them. Not all packs are as fortunate as mine to have all these amenities."

My jealousy eased at his words and I blushed with embarrassment over my outburst. Killian came up behind me and started kissing my neck.

"You are ours and we are yours, darling," he murmured to me. "Always and forever."

My pussy clenched at his words and I could feel slick already start to drip out at his comforting words. It seemed like I was always desiring them. I wasn't worried anymore about pregnancy. Duncan informed me that omegas could only get pregnant during their heat cycle and so far, I hadn't had another one.

"Hold on guys, I need to choose my ice cream first before we do anything," I laughed out as Kayden started pulling my dress down.

"Of course," said Lucien, handing me the ice cream menu before kneeling down between my legs. I opened the menu with shaky hands as he moved my underwear to the side and started lapping up all the slick I had formed.

Kayden pulled my breasts free from my dress and started sucking on both my nipples simultaneously, squeezing my breasts together. Killian licked and sucked at the sensitive spot on my neck. I quickly chose a random ice cream and gave my order to Duncan, who went out to get it.

Kayden laid me down on the soft cushions and removed my dress fully. Lucien kneeled between my splayed legs and continued eating me out. Warm sunlight flooded the room, and for a moment, I could believe I was in heaven.

I was surrounded by three alphas, all using their tongues and fingers to bring me pleasure repeatedly.

Duncan walked back in, carrying a tray laden with ice cream, chocolate syrup, whipped cream and strawberries.

"Time to eat ice cream, guys," he said.

Killian grabbed a scoop of ice cream and rubbed it all over my breasts. I gasped at the coldness of it and he chuckled darkly. He took one breast into his warm mouth and cleaned it off, sucking away every last drop as Kayden did the same on the other side.

Lucien drizzled chocolate syrup all over my pussy, rubbing it in and mixing with my slick. Then he dived in and lapped it all up, slurping away with his tongue.

"Don't worry, love, I didn't forget your order," Duncan said with his dick out and covered in strawberry ice cream and whipped cream.

I giggled and opened my mouth, accepting my sweet treat. I licked away at his cock like it was a popsicle and the ice cream was absolutely delicious. It was buttery soft in my mouth and I could taste a hint of saltiness from Duncan's pre-cum.

I moaned at the yumminess and decadence of it all.

Chapter 16

Kayden

I switched places with Lucien, pulling off my pants and letting out my dick.

It was time to formally mark our omega and, as top alpha, the honor was mine to mark her first. I slowly pushed into her slick entrance, watching her eyes light up in pleasure.

She wasn't even in heat, but her channel was wet for me. I grunted in male satisfaction as I entered her fully, balls deep in her pussy. The other alphas continued pleasuring her as I rutted into her deeply.

I slowed down my pace, forcing myself to calm down. This was a sacred ritual, and I wasn't about to rush it. I thrust into her more slowly and purposefully. I rubbed against her g spot with my dick, watching her twist and thrash about with the powerful sensations.

I nodded toward Killian and Lucien and they each took one of her arms and lifted her upper body up towards me. My dick remained in her pussy as she was presented to me. Duncan moved her fiery hair to the side, baring her neck.

She looked around in confusion.

"Do you, Adrianna of the Greenwich pack, accept Kayden of the Bloodmoon pack, to be one of your fated mates?" I asked her formally, thrusting deep into her with each word.

Her eyes softened, and she gazed at me with love. And without hesitation, she said, "I do."

My heart burst at her words, and I leaned over and grasped the side of her neck with my mouth. I allowed my wolf's fangs to release, biting into her deeply, drawing blood. She gasped out in pain, until my wolf saliva mixed in and numbed the bite, sending her into a state of rapture.

She screamed out and came hard on my dick, spasming over and over. Her pussy clamped down and squeezed my shaft harder than I had ever felt and gushes of slick poured out of her. I roared out and slammed into her hard and fast. There was no holding back now.

She was officially my mate in every way that mattered.

My balls tightened up, and I shot my load into her, my dick pulsating powerfully. I never came this hard in my life. My knot swelled up instantly, locking us together so tight it almost hurt. I licked at the droplets of blood around her mated mark, sealing up her wound.

I hugged her close to me as we remained knotted together. The others congratulated us, eagerly awaiting their turn as they cleaned up the remaining ice cream mess. I looked into her beautiful clear eyes and stroked her hair.

"How are you feeling, baby?" I asked her.

"On top of the world," she replied dreamily.

I kissed her soft lips thoroughly. Her courage and inner strength amazed me to no end. She had faced so much trauma and was able to heal from it and walk away without a single thought to it. She had grown up unaware of her nature, but then fully accepted it without breaking her stride.

She looked so delicate from the outside but was made of steel from the inside.

We were so damn lucky to have her and I would make sure we were worthy of being her mates.

"You know, your family and friends are welcome here anytime you want. I want you to feel like you're home," I told her in earnest.

She bit her lip and looked away, her eyes filling with tears. "Jess is no longer my friend, and I'm not ready yet to forgive my parents for not telling me the truth about who I am. I still need more time."

I gently wiped away her tears, wanting to throttle the bitch who refused to help my mate in her time of need. I masked my anger and comforted Adrianna.

"Of course, baby. Whenever you're ready."

My knot released her, and I set her down gently on the soft cushions. I grabbed some wet towels Duncan had thoughtfully brought along with the ice cream and started wiping her down. I cleaned away the remnants of ice cream and chocolate syrup from her body.

She looked at me with her heart in her eyes and I felt such a strong desire to cherish and love on her.

The others returned, all the ice cream completely cleaned away.

"Are you ready to continue your tour, baby?" I asked her with a wide grin.

"Yes," she said happily, mirroring my grin and getting up. "But first, I'm gonna need some clothes," she said teasingly.

The others laughed as if she had told a world-renowned joke, and I smirked at them. They were vying for her favor so they could be next to mark her.

Killian quickly produced her dress and helped her into it, and Lucien held open the door. We made our way out, thanking the owner as we exited. Adrianna blushed cutely and couldn't make eye contact with the owner.

I chuckled.

Adrianna

It felt like I was doing a walk of shame as we left the ice cream shop.

Everyone probably knew what we were up to. My face was on fire and, thankfully, we left quickly and got back into the little golf cart. This time, Duncan sat in the front beside me and directed us to the next stop on our tour.

"This is one of my favorite places to be," he said shyly. "Besides being with you, of course." He added hastily, to my amusement.

We had stopped in front of a grand library, constructed in the likes of the Greek Parthenon, complete with white marble and statues. My jaw dropped at the magnificence of the building. It was clearly built with care and an artist's eye.

"I am a patron here. Many packs from around the country come to visit and read our extensive collection of books," Duncan continued on, bolstered by my amazed reaction.

We stepped into the cool, quiet interior of the library and the smell of books brought a wave of homesickness to me. Tears filled my eyes as memories flooded back to me. My dad used to take me and my sisters to the library every week when we were kids.

Kayden was right.

It was probably time to reach out to my parents and make amends. But for now, I blinked away my tears, determined to enjoy Duncan's portion of this, so far amazing, tour.

We passed by many book sections of the library, making our way to a long winding staircase that led to darkness above.

"Where are we going?" I whispered to Duncan, not wanting to disturb the readers sitting about.

"There is a somewhat private reading area I want to show you," he replied noncommittally.

Duncan took my hand and led me up the foreboding staircase. Killian held my other hand below, ensuring I kept my balance. I did not see where Kayden and Lucien went off to.

It was just me, Duncan and Killian going up the never ending staircase together.

Eventually, we reached the top and stepped into a beautiful, dark velvet room. It reminded me of a dimly lit fortune teller's cave. I could even see black tassel curtains. There was a balcony that extended out over the rest of the library.

I stepped out and gripped the railing, viewing the readers and the books far below.

Suddenly, I felt cool air around my bottom. I gasped and looked around. Duncan had lifted my dress up and was gazing at my bottom. I opened my mouth, but before I could say anything, he put his finger to my lips, shushing me. He motioned down below to the unaware readers, and I got the message loud and clear.

I had to stay quiet or risk the entire library looking up and seeing my exposed bottom.

The thrill of secrecy sent flutters of excitement through my belly and between my legs. Duncan started massaging my butt, and Killian came around to my front and pulled down the top of my dress. My breasts and bottom were completely bare now.

Killian flashed an evil grin before reaching between my legs and massaging my clit.

I bit my tongue to hold back my moans. I was loud during sex, and he knew it. Having to stay quiet was killing me.

I decided I shouldn't suffer on my own. I undid his suit pants button and zipper and pulled his cock free. None of them seemed to wear any underwear, and that was fine by me. He closed his eyes as I started pulling on his dick. I reached between my legs and gathered slick to moisten his dick and make it easier to jerk him off.

"Fuck," Duncan breathed into my ear, slipping a finger into my butthole.

Killian's eyes shot open at the sensation of my slick rubbing onto his cock, and he let out a spurt of pre-cum. He grabbed my hand and sucked off every finger, devouring my slick from my hand.

I held back my giggle at the ticklish sensation, remembering to stay quiet.

Killian lifted me up and wrapped my legs around his waist. I lined up his cock to my entrance and let gravity do the rest. Slowly, I sank down onto his cock all the way to the hilt. Behind me, Duncan started inserting a second finger, stretching me out and ensuring I was ready for his very thick cock.

I kissed Killian as silently as I could, wanting desperately to scream out as he started thrusting into me.

Duncan removed his fingers, and then I felt the head of his cock nudge at my ass. He spread my cheeks wide, and I felt a twinge of nervousness. His cock was very thick and wide, and I wasn't sure if I could take it back there. He felt me tense up and stroked my hair, murmuring against my ear, soothing away my fears.

Slowly, my butt unclenched and he started pushing his way in. By the time he was fully in, I was stretched out so wide and felt so full I could barely breathe. Killian and Duncan started fucking me in tandem. I stuffed a fist into my mouth to keep from crying out.

Duncan reached around my waist and placed his hand on my clit, rubbing it furiously as they both thrusted into me at the same time. Slick dropped out of me and onto the beautiful velvet floor.

I reached over and bit Killian's shoulder with my human teeth, marking him as best as I could. I felt his cock spasm inside me, and he looked at me with his wild wolf's eyes. They were glowing as he barely held onto his human side.

"Do you, Adrianna of the Greenwich pack, accept Killian of the Bloodmoon pack, to be one of your fated mates?" He whispered to me harshly through clenched teeth.

"I do," I breathed back, bracing myself for his bite.

He swiftly clamped down onto my neck and I gasped as his fangs pierced through, marking me as his mate. The pain disappeared quickly and in its place was the indescribable pleasure. My pussy clenched, and I came over and over, losing count of how many times I reached my climax.

I was barely aware of Duncan whispering his vows in my ear.

Chapter 17

Adrianna

"Do you, Adrianna of the Greenwich pack, accept Duncan of the Bloodmoon pack, to be one of your fated mates?"

"I do, I do, I do," I moaned out, forgetting to be quiet and excited for another mating bite.

Duncan did not disappoint in the slightest. He licked the other side of my neck, sending shivers down my spine. His wolf's fangs snapped out and he bit down deep, drawing my blood into his mouth and releasing his numbing wolf saliva into my bite.

Ecstasy shot through my veins. I lost track of time and space, floating through a haze of unending orgasms.

I felt their knots swell up inside me and jet after jet of hot cum loaded up inside me. Their fangs were still buried on each side of my neck and I was well and truly claimed. I reached my hands up and ran my fingers through Duncan's short buzz cut and Killian's unruly curls.

Killian released my neck first, licking my wound and sealing it with his tongue, and Duncan followed suit. Their knots were still swelled up inside me and would be for some time.

My stomach growled loudly in hunger, and my eyes widened in shock and embarrassment. I couldn't stop it at all. I peeked over the balcony railing and thankfully no one was looking up or had noticed what we had been up to.

I motioned to Killian to scoot back into the room as our little adventure was coming to a close. I wasn't an exhibitionist, and I had already risked too much.

He grinned and did an awkward shuffle with Duncan, both of them still locked in me, and we reached the privacy of the dark room. They tipped us over and we landed on the fluffy, dark cushions.

These omega rooms were really amazing and came in handy, no pun intended.

"I am hungry," I announced out loud, relieved to finally speak and break our silence.

"We figured," said Killian with a wry grin. "That's where Kayden and Lucien went, to bring lunch after our mating."

"Lucien drew the short stick, so we got to mate with you first." Duncan added.

I rolled my eyes at their antics. For all their big, scruffy exteriors, they were still little boys at heart. Everything was a game of competition between them. I acted annoyed, but it was amusing to watch and it made me feel so special about the way they fought over me.

Duncan and Killian's knots released me simultaneously, and they withdrew from me carefully. Duncan went to get the never-ending towels to help me clean up, and Killian prepared an area for our arriving food.

This was such a cool place to picnic in, so cozy and isolated from the rest of the world.

"Do you have a phone on you?" I asked Killian. "I think I want to call my parents now."

He wore a surprised look on his face, but handed me his phone. I quickly dialed Momma's number and held my breath as the phone rang.

"Hello? Who's this?" Momma said. Her warm, familiar voice healed the holes in my heart.

"It's me, Adrianna," I said, my voice cracking with emotion. It felt like ages since I had spoken to them, after everything that had happened.

"Oh! Adrianna! I've been worried sick. I've missed you soo much. Where are you? I'm so sorry for everything that's happened," she tripped over her words, desperate to get everything out.

I laughed, "I'm okay, Momma. I'm with my pack now and I'm fine. Everything is okay and I forgive you, don't worry about it."

She sobbed on her end of the phone and I wished I had called her sooner.

All the anger I had felt towards them before was gone. I understood now why they had hidden me. Omegas had it rough in the world and they had wanted me to experience the options of life. While I still didn't agree with their methods, even I could see that they did what they did out of love.

We talked about anything and everything until Kayden and Lucien arrived with large, fancy boxes of steaming food. My mouth watered, and I quickly hung up, assuring her I would call again soon.

"Ooooh, it smells so good!" I exclaimed, clapping my hands in excitement.

"We weren't sure which type of foods you liked, so we ordered the best from each restaurant," Kayden stated proudly.

My mouth gaped open as Lucien started pulling out Chinese food and Mexican cuisine. Kayden set out Italian and Ethiopian dishes, all vegetarian. I peeked in the bag and saw some sandwiches.

My stomach rumbled loudly to my chagrin, and everyone laughed.

Paper plates were passed around, and my plate was loaded up with a little of everything. Killian had lit candles all around so we could see, and everything felt so ethereal and otherworldly. The thick velvet curtains to the balcony were closed so we could laugh and speak loudly without disturbing the rest of the library.

I looked around at all of their faces, and my heart felt like it could burst with joy. I was almost fully mated to all of them and having the time of my life.

Lucien

I watched the way Adrianna laughed and enjoyed her food with a gusto.

I tracked her every movement, handing her napkins and condiments before she could ask. My dick was rock hard as I saw the three alpha marks on her neck. And the empty spot just above her collarbone, just waiting for my fangs to sink in and claim her.

I was so fucking mad at drawing the short stick and losing to Duncan and Killian. But at least, when it was my turn to mark her, I would have her all to myself and didn't have to share.

She didn't notice the way I followed her with my eyes or the desire burning within them. She would have run screaming in the opposite direction if she could read my thoughts right now.

I remembered the way she loved my present above all the rest.

It more than made up for the bunny shit on my favorite shirt. The fucker wouldn't stay in the basket, but she seemed to love the creepy creature. To me, bunnies were for eating, not living with.

I kept those thoughts to myself as I watched her spill ketchup on her cleavage.

Fast as a snake, I swiped it off with my finger and popped it into my mouth, looking her in the eye. She blushed furiously and looked away, focusing back on her grilled sandwich and whatever lie Killian was boasting about.

I let it go. For now.

But very soon, I was going to rut into her and mate with her and she would have eyes only for me at that moment.

We stayed at the little alcove for quite some time, eating dessert and just lounging about. I checked my phone frequently, ensuring everything was still on track for the remainder of the date. Once sunset hit, it was time to wrap up and head out.

"Where are we going now?" Adrianna asked, a twinkle in her eye.

"I arranged a surprise for you on the hill," I replied mysteriously. "But we're going to have to head out now if we're going to make it on time."

"We'll let you two go on ahead while we finish up cleaning here," Kayden offered graciously. The others groaned at being assigned tasks and not spending time with Adrianna.

I glared at the greedy fuckers. It was finally my turn and the least they could do was not complain.

I ignored them and focused my attentions on the beautiful, glowing Adrianna. After eating and resting, she was more than ready for another outing. And she beamed at me.

I felt a little nervous, unsure how to handle all the open love and happiness she exuded constantly.

It was not possible for a person to be so happy and light all the time, yet Adrianna was a living and breathing example. Even when she was healing from her horrific attack, she only had positive words and feelings to share.

It was very jarring, coming from my world of ice and darkness.

We left the library together and went to the little cart. The sun was setting, and we made the short drive to the hill right as the sun let out its last rays. I grabbed the basket I had left in the back of the cart and we made our way up the hill.

I spread out a thick blanket from the basket on the top of the hill, and Adrianna wandered around smelling the flowers. I finished setting up, placing candles on the borders of the blanket and tracking the way the omega's hips swayed with every step. I checked my phone; it was time.

"Come here, little omega, it's about to start," I said gruffly, nervousness coating the back of my throat.

She blushed, removing her flats and stepped barefoot onto the blanket. My cock twitched at the sight of her elegantly arched feet with her painted, sparkly red nails.

Every inch of her was so fucking perfect, I did not deserve to be in her presence. Someone as scarred as me, on the inside and out, should be kept far away from an angel like her.

And yet somehow, a monster like me could hold her and touch her. I was so damn fucking lucky. I would not mess this up. I reached out a hand towards her and she grasped it eagerly. I sat her in my lap, facing her away from me. Her back was to my chest, and she looked on ahead in confusion.

"Wait for it," I whispered in her ear.

Suddenly, the night sky lit up with a bang and colorful fireworks illuminated the darkness. Adrianna squealed in surprise and clapped her hands in happiness.

"This is amazing," she shouted back to me.

The fireworks spelled out her name in giant gold letters:

A D R I A N N A

She looked back at me with wide eyes. "How?"

"The fireworks are for you, little omega," I replied, relieved at her excitement. I wanted to end the date memorably, and I was nervous she was going to hate it.

She clasped her hands to her heart and oohed at the colorful displays of hearts and roses. I grunted in satisfaction. The firework guys were worth the money we paid them, I had to admit.

But we weren't here for just the fireworks.

I slowly reached around and pulled her clasped hands apart. I needed access to her large tits. I pulled down the top of her dress down her shoulders and let it fall down to her waist.

The night was warm, but her exposed pink nipples still hardened as the air touched it. I cupped her tits in my hands, rolling the tips between my fingers. Her breasts were so large, they over spilled in my grasp. She let her head fall back to my chest and relaxed in my hold, watching the fireworks with a dreamy look upon her face.

Fuck.

Her unabashed relaxation into her pleasure was so fucking sexy. Her long lashes fluttered at the fireworks and her full lips were curved into a content smile.

Chapter 18

Adrianna

This was such an amazing day, it didn't feel real. I was convinced I was dreaming at this point. I lay back in Lucien's arms, enjoying the way he was fondling my breasts. Twinges of pleasure ran through my body.

The fireworks display was breathtaking and heartbreakingly romantic. The way it spelled out my name was so thoughtful and sweet. I did not expect such beautiful gestures from the scarred alpha. Everyone believed him to be damaged and broken, but I did not see him that way.

Yes, he was more careful than most and spoke little, but I could see his love for me and dedication to his pack in everything that he did. I believe he felt his emotions more deeply than others, but hid them.

My wandering thoughts slipped away as he reached his hand between my legs, hiking my dress up and casually slipping a finger inside my pussy. I moaned at the deliciousness of it all.

He massaged my channel with his finger, and we continued watching the fireworks above us. Then he lay me down on the blanket and replaced his finger with his mouth.

"I love eating you out, little omega. Your pussy tastes like caramel," he rasped against me. I blushed at his explicit words and unexpected compliment.

My embarrassment quickly left me and I spread my legs out wider, giving him deeper access with his tongue. He thrust his tongue in and out of my slick hole, a preview of what was to come.

He reached up and continued playing with my nipples. His tongue swirled around my clit, and I shuddered at the sensation. I couldn't wait anymore. I needed his cock in me.

"I need your knot, Lucien," I gasped out boldly.

His eyes widened at my words.

"Turn over, little omega." He said, giving my pussy a final lick.

Hurt flashed in my eyes at his words. *Why did he never want to see my face while we had sex?* Now that I thought about it, I remembered every time we had sex he was always at my back, avoiding my gaze.

"Why?" I asked him, hurt in my tone.

"I never fuck face to face." He replied harshly, his emotionless mask snapped firmly back in place.

"Well then, I guess we're not fucking then," I retorted, copying his crude language. The fireworks continued flashing overhead, a mockery of the now turned sour date.

"I'll be the judge of that," he said lasciviously, licking my pussy from top to bottom again.

"No, Lucien!" I said, pulling away quickly and closing my legs shut. I adjusted my dress to cover myself up, suddenly feeling exposed.

"Why do you shut yourself away like this? Why can't you open up to me?" I asked outright, determined to get to the bottom of this once and for all.

He turned his face away, getting ready to leave, like he did the last time I asked about his scar. But not this time. I didn't go through hell and back just to get half assed responses from him again.

I grabbed his face in my hands and looked him in the eyes, stroking his scar with my hand. "I love you, Lucien. Do you hear me? I love you!"

Pain filled his eyes at my words and he was stunned speechless. "No one has ever said that to me before." He admitted quietly.

I was shocked by his admission. "Surely, your mother must've told you that every day." I thought out slowly.

He laughed bitterly. "She's the one who gave me my scar."

I stared at him in disbelief. In my horrified silence, he finally let out his story, outlining the terrible details of his life in brief, curt sentences.

"When I was born, it was clearly evident that my mother's husband could not be my father," he said, gesturing to his pale features.

"It turned out she had been cheating on him and so he left her. She had still loved him though and blamed my existence as the reason he left," he continued on, staring off into the distance.

"She beat me daily and would lock me in a closet for hours at a time, get shitfaced drunk and cry nonstop. When I was eight, she carved at my face with a knife, desperate to change my appearance. In her drunken haze, she believed that would bring her love back." He said softly, lost in the memories of his past.

I held my hands to my mouth in shock, tears filling my eyes for that terrified little boy. My heart wrenched at the cruelties he had endured. I wanted to strangle that sorry of an excuse mother he had.

"Eventually, I ran away when I was twelve and never looked back." He finished up quickly, bringing us back to the present moment.

"So you see, little omega, every woman I've been with has requested that I turn my face away during sex. My face has been unlovable by any woman since the day I was born."

"No, don't say that. Never say that," I whispered thickly, tears blurring my vision.

I reached over and wrapped my arms around his neck, showering his face with kisses through my tears.

"Your mother was an unhinged, mentally unstable person who should not have been allowed to take you home. I am so sorry the people around you failed you," I said, deadly serious and intent on making him understand my point.

"And those other women were vapid, shallow bitches who don't represent the rest of us," I continued on, straddling his lap and looking him dead in the eye.

I moved my hips, gyrating and grinding against him seductively. His face lightened at my words and I could see a weight lifted off of him. He held his head up higher and looked ten years younger. The lines of his mask had melted away.

"And now, I believe we have a mating ceremony to conduct," I said suggestively, hiking my dress up around my waist and baring my lower body.

He grinned at and grabbed my hips, pulling me closer, "My little omega is correct. We have much to conduct."

He pulled his cock out of his pants and grasped my butt with both hands. There was no more time for games. I was already dripping with slick. I gazed deep into his pale eyes as he lowered me onto his hard cock.

His thickness filled me up and he thrust into me with an intensity, fucking me hard and fast. He held me close, bouncing me up and down, murmuring words of love and praise.

"Oh, Adrianna," he said in wonderment, never breaking eye contact with me.

Hearing my name pass his lips for the first time sent me over the edge. I screamed out my orgasm, clenching his dick hard and releasing slick. He roared out and held my bottom firmly, grounding me against him.

His fangs shot out, and he had to speak his vows around them.

"Do you, Adrianna of the Greenwich pack, accept Lucien of the Bloodmoon pack, to be your final fated mate?"

"I accept you, Lucien, to be my final fated mate." I gasped out, meaning every word.

He slowly tilted my head to the side and I closed my eyes, bracing myself for the bite. But I did not feel pain as he gently slid his fangs in, immediately releasing his wolf's saliva to numb the bite. I moaned out as I got my final hit of the nirvana drug.

I had never done drugs in my life, but if I had, I would imagine that it would feel like this. I moaned out as my pussy spasmed helplessly on his dick. His bite sent me over the edge again and again and I rode the wave.

He couldn't hold out anymore and came while still buried deep in my neck and in my channel. He released spurt after spurt of fluid, and I could feel it filling me up. His knot swelled up thick, stretching me out even further and connecting us as one.

Our fast breaths eventually slowed, and I put my forehead on his, enjoying seeing him during this vulnerable time. He smiled at me and wiped at a droplet of blood on my neck.

"We are officially fated mates, little omega." He said happily.

I placed my hand on my chest in wonderment. I could feel a tentative bond connecting me to all four alphas at once. It was a line, radiating out from my heart and branching out in four different directions.

"Do you feel that?" I breathed out in wonderment.

He closed his eyes and inhaled deeply, filling his chest with air. "I do, little omega."

I sighed in satisfaction, burrowing against his chest for warmth. The night air had turned chilly.

Chapter 19

Adrianna

After we made it back to the house, I soaked in the tub for hours, refilling it with hot water each time. I marveled at the new bond I felt in my chest. I would never feel alone anymore. I had four alpha presences to comfort me at any time.

At the present moment, however, I needed some alone time. The date was wonderful, but I was drained and needed time to relax and think by myself.

Something was changing in my body again. I could feel copious amounts of slick being released, and I was feeling slightly feverish. My next heat was coming on strong. The symptoms felt stronger than the last time I was in heat.

I had to ignore it for now. There was no way I was going to get rutted into until this heat passed. I did not want to have a baby yet. I would just have to deal with the pain when it came and wait until it passed. Even if it took days.

Duncan had told me regular omega heats could last up to a week. They were surprised my last one had been so short, but it was probably because I hadn't been around alpha pheromones my whole life.

I felt a twinge of a cramp in my lower belly, but brushed it off as I got out of the bath and toweled off. I dressed in some silky pajamas and made my way to my bed. Or should I say our bed?

All four alphas lay sprawled out on the massive bed, leaving a space for me in the center. I crawled over them and nestled cozily in the middle. I was surrounded on all sides and I had never felt more safe and wanted in my life. I closed my eyes and drifted off to sleep.

Duncan

I awoke to the potent scent of caramel. It was emanating from Adrianna in powerful waves. I inhaled deeply through my nose and noticed hints of the sweet scent of slick.

Fuck.

She was in the middle of heat and needed knots. I furrowed my brow.

But why didn't she tell us?

She must be in agony now, based on the amounts I could smell in the air alone.

Sure enough, I glanced over at her sleeping face and saw her brow furrowed in pain. She whimpered in her sleep and curled into a ball, clutching her stomach.

My face softened with sympathy, and I reached over to wake her up. And to give her my knot so she could have some relief. There was no need for her to suffer like this anymore.

She was mated now. I thought to myself, my cock twitching in anticipation.

I gently brushed Adrianna's hair out of her face.

"Love, wake up. I'm here." I whispered softly.

She stirred and groaned in pain, blinking the sleep out of her eyes. She sat up slowly in confusion, holding her stomach. Then awareness hit her and she looked at me with panicked eyes.

"No, no, stay away from me!" she shouted wildly, arms outstretched. I looked at her in shock.

What the hell?

The others got up, woken up by her shout. Then the scent of her heat hit them and the room was suddenly filled with four horny alphas, ready to rut their omega.

She backed up slowly until she hit the headboard behind her. Her arms were still outstretched, and she looked at each of us with wild eyes.

"Love, what's wrong? We know you're in heat. Why won't you accept our knots this time?" I asked her.

She took a calming breath and spoke, "I can get through this heat without knots. Just stay away from me, and I can do this."

Kayden spoke up, confusion also written all over his face. "But why would you want to? You mated us and we can help you."

Tears filled her eyes and overflowed down her face. "I don't want to get pregnant. Last heat cycle I got lucky, but I can't risk it again."

Understanding filled me with her words. I had explained to her that omegas could only get pregnant during their heat cycles. I guess I forgot to mention the bit about contraceptives.

I threw my head back and laughed. Everyone looked at me in confusion.

"Oh, love! I forgot to tell you about the birth control for omegas. You can take a pill during your heat to avoid pregnancies if that is what you really wish. I have some for you in my office," I explained, careful not to omit any details this time.

Killian ran out to fetch them.

Her face relaxed in relief, and she let out a wavering smile. "Thank god! I didn't know how much longer I could wait out the pain."

Kayden took on a serious tone. "Omegas have died before from not getting knots in time during their heats. Nothing is worth your life, baby."

Adrianna's eyes widened in shock. "I had no idea. I was terrified at the thought of being a mother. I definitely don't feel ready yet," she admitted quietly.

Killian returned with the pills and a glass of water. She accepted them graciously and downed a pill swiftly.

"Well, now that we got all that sorted out, who do you want first, baby?" Kayden said, pulling out his cock from his pants and letting it stand to attention in front of her.

Not to be outdone, I quickly unzipped and pulled out my own cock, pumping its thick length to harden it to its full glory.

"Yes, love, which cock do you need first?" I added, expanding her options.

Lucien and Killian followed suit, and she had a row of alpha cocks presented in front of her, waiting for her choice.

She put a finger to her lips and looked over at each of us in amusement. She hummed in indecisiveness and my balls tightened up. Then she got a mischievous twinkle in her eyes and made her announcement.

"Well, I simply cannot choose a winner from any of you. Therefore, you must all give me your cocks at the same time." She proclaimed royally. Despite her grand words, her cheeks were stained dark red in shyness.

The room was dead silent for a beat as everyone processed her words.

Then a flurry of activity ensued as everyone burst into action.

I reached her first and brought her to the center of the bed. Kayden grabbed pillows and propped her up for the view of everyone. Killian stripped off her clothes and Lucien spread her legs wide, exposing her pussy to the room.

She giggled at our speed and intensity, but she just lit a fire in every alpha in the room. Her giggles turned into gasps and moans of delight as I dived between her legs and started lapping up all of her released slick.

Kayden and Lucien played with her tits, as I prepared her pussy for all the knots she was going to receive today.

Killian replaced the pillows behind her back with his body. He stretched out her asshole while I worked on her front.

"She's ready back here," Killian announced, removing his fingers and replacing them with the head of his cock.

I slurped at her clit and looked her in the eye. "Are you ready for a dick over here, love?"

She mewled in frustration, but I needed to hear her bold words again. I smiled and resumed my teasing with my tongue. She thrust her hips up in desperation.

"Yes! Yes! I am ready for a dick in my pussy," she shouted out, screwing her eyes shut in embarrassment.

I grunted in satisfaction, pulling back and lining up my cock at her entrance. I slowly pushed in, matching the pace of Killian at her rear. Her moans of satisfaction were quickly drowned out as she accepted Kayden's dick in her mouth.

Lucien, feeling left out, nudged at her hands with his cock until she gripped it and started pumping.

I pushed all the way in and felt a new gush of slick release all over my member. She popped Kayden's cock out of her mouth to gasp at me. "Harder, Duncan."

That was all the encouragement I needed. I rutted into her fast and hard, in tandem with Killian. I felt her channel squeezing and milking me. I held out as long as I could, desperate to give her the relief she craved.

I lost the fight, and I came with a roar, spurting deep inside her. My cock throbbed with each release of fluid and my knot started to swell up.

Killian increased his tempo before my knot became too large for him to continue rutting her. He came seconds after me, and our knots locked her in, providing her temporary relief from her heat.

Chapter 20

Adrianna

Kayden withdrew from my mouth before he came, murmuring about me needing his knot elsewhere.

I smiled in relieved satisfaction. The two knots already in me had stabilized my heat, and my pain was long gone. But I knew it would return soon.

For now, I just enjoyed the closeness of Duncan and Killian. I snuggled in closer to their warmth, my eyes drifting shut as I went back to sleep.

I awoke to find Lucien had gone out and fetched me some breakfast. I would need my strength for the rest of my heat. I scarfed down the food, also from a restaurant. Killian really needed to get back into the kitchen. His cooking skills were much better, in my opinion.

I spent the rest of the next few days in and out of heat.

I was knotted many times and the other times were spent in deep conversation and laughter. I had never experienced such a depth of love before. My heart felt like it could burst with emotion.

Honestly, life couldn't get any better than this.

A couple of days later, I was sitting on the beach with my alphas for breakfast. It was magical, with the wind flying in my hair and Duncan feeding me biscuits.

The sun has just begun to rise, casting a soft, golden glow across the tranquil beach. Before me lay a breakfast feast, an array of delicious treats that the alphas and I shared. Laughter and chatter filled the air as my four alphas sat around me, their smiles warming my heart.

"Eat up, love," said Duncan, laughing as I swiped at a pesky bee.

Kayden cleared his throat, drawing my attention. His gaze was intense, his hand holding a small velvet box.

Duncan drew me up to my feet.

"What's going on?" I asked in confusion.

Then, as one, all the alphas kneeled on one knee at my feet. Kayden spoke up.

"Adrianna, we have already been officially mated according to our customs. But we also wanted to honor the life that you grew up in and the world in which you are most familiar. That being said, would you do us the greatest honor of marrying us?" He said solemnly, his heart in his eyes.

Kayden opened the box dramatically, revealing an exquisite ring. I squealed and clapped my hands with joy. This was better than any rom com I could have ever watched.

"Yes!" I burst out, happiness exploding in my chest. He slid the ring onto my finger, and I marveled at its beauty. There were four tiny gemstones all grouped together into one ring. A diamond, an emerald, a ruby, and a sapphire.

It was beautiful and unique, a perfect representation of our union.

I kissed each of them, overwhelmed by their thoughtfulness and gesture.

"Would you like to get married today, baby?" He asked me.

I gasped in excitement.

"I'm gonna need some time to do my makeup to match the dress, but of course!" I exclaimed. The beach was filled with chuckles at my words.

"Take all the time you need. The ceremony will begin at sunset." Kayden assured me with a grin.

I gazed at myself in the full-length mirror and pinched myself to make sure I wasn't dreaming. I looked like a vision in a stunning white dress that the alphas provided for me. One of the maids helped me put my hair up in a fancy French updo. The engagement ring sparkled on my finger, and I was ready to be married.

I felt a twinge of sadness that my mother was not here to see me in my dress. I straightened my necklace and comforted myself that I would soon visit her after I settled fully into my life here.

I walked out of the room and made my way down the stairs to the front door. My long train rustled behind me with every step that I took. I reached the front door, unsure of what to expect. Kayden had only said to be here at sunset and nothing more.

The front door opened, revealing my father.

"Dad!" I exclaimed in happiness. "How are you here!?"

He was dressed in a dark brown plaid suit and had a twinkle in his eye.

"You didn't think I was going to miss my eldest's wedding now, did you?" He replied cheerfully.

I pulled him in for a long hug, inhaling his familiar coffee and books scent.

"And Momma?" I asked him hopefully.

"Waiting with the rest outside," he said reassuringly. "Now, let's see you get married."

He held out his arm and handed me a bouquet of flowers. He led me out the front door, and I stared in awe at what my mates had done for me.

The yard was beautifully decorated with white silks and flowers hanging from erected poles scattered throughout. I stepped onto a white aisle runner that led to an arched overhang where all four of my mates stood, waiting for me with huge grins on their faces.

There were a few people in the audience. Mostly the staff from the house, but I spied my mom's curly red bun from where I stood, and I smiled with happiness. I also saw Amber sitting beside her, and my heart warmed. To my shock, I spied Jess in the crowd as well.

Music played, and we started down the pathway. Everyone stood up and turned to me. I was smiling so hard my cheeks were hurting, and I finally reached the end of the pathway to my mates and the marriage officiant.

I clasped each of their hands in turn, and we said our marriage vows.

Kayden was first.

"Adrianna, I promise to love and protect you, always. My body is your shield. I will happily slay any enemies who dare stand before you until the day I die," he vowed to me.

Duncan stepped forward next. "Adrianna, from the moment I laid eyes on you, you captured my heart. Your sweet, gentle soul inspires me to be the best mate that you deserve. I look forward to spending the rest of my days with you."

I tried to keep my happy tears from running down my made-up face, but I lost that fight.

Killian strode up for his turn. "Adrianna, meeting you was the best thing that has ever happened to me. You are the flaming sun I live for now. I see my life in your eyes. You are my today and all of my tomorrows."

I held my hands to my heart, absorbing the powerful words being spoken to me.

Lucien came up last and said his vows. "I've never known love until you, Adrianna. I will honor and guard your heart for the rest of my life. Your heart is now my heart, and I vow to cherish and protect it."

I choked out my vows, knowing there was no way I could top their gallant promises.

They smiled, understanding the emotion behind my unintelligible words. Everything was a blur as I turned to the cheering audience, officially married in the eyes of werewolves and humans alike.

An outdoor evening party ensued, and I got a chance to catch up with Momma and Amber.

"Adrianna, you look stunning!" squealed out Amber.

"Aw, thank you!" I replied, laughing.

I hugged Momma close, happy to finally see her in person.

Jess appeared from behind Amber, wringing her hands and shuffling her feet nervously. Amber pushed her forward towards me and nudged her to speak.

"Adrianna, I'm so sorry. I didn't mean to treat you that way. I was just so jealous of omegas, and I judged you harshly. You didn't deserve my hatred." She said tearfully, full of sorrow.

I paused for a beat and then spoke.

"Girl, you better not be crying on my wedding day," I said with a smile. The past was the past, and I wanted to keep it there.

Jess looked up at me hopefully and then grinned with happiness after seeing my smile. She hugged me, promising all the ways she would make things up with me.

I danced and laughed with my mates and my family, enjoying all the wonderful food that was laid out on a long table. The alphas flirted with me outrageously, each trying to outdo the last. I laughed at their antics, feeling cherished and loved beyond words.

My world was complete, and my life was changed forever.

Epilogue

Three years later...

Adrianna

I grimaced as baby girl kicked me in the ribs again. I was two weeks overdue, and she still didn't want to make her appearance. Instead, she preferred kicking me as soon as I got myself into a comfortable position lounging on the sofa.

"Lucien," I called out, rubbing my tummy to calm her. "I forgot my water in the kitchen. Could you grab it for me, please?"

"Sure thing, little omega." He returned with a cup of water in his hand. He handed it to me, but I fumbled the glass, my fingers slipping on its surface.

The cup fell with a shattering crash, spraying water everywhere.

"Shit," I sighed, getting to my feet.

Pop.

Liquid gushed out of me in a torrent, soaking my legs and the floor beneath me. *Double shit.*

"My water just broke," I gasped out to Lucien, wide eyed.

We both glanced out the window. The sun was setting and nightfall was rapidly approaching.

"The eclipse is tonight," I said with dread and sadness. The first contraction hit me like a wave and I groaned through it.

"No, no, no, it wasn't supposed to be like this," I cried out in pain.

Kayden and the rest of the alphas came bursting into the room, alarmed by the crash.

"She's gone into labor," Lucien informed them swiftly. "Prepare the supplies. We're about to deliver a little omega."

Several hours later, I gave a final mighty push, putting everything I had into it. I screamed out in agony, my womb contracting horribly. And then I heard it.

The tiny wavering cry of a newborn baby and my eyes flooded with tears. Kayden handed her to me, a tiny bundle all wrapped up, and I could barely make out her face. I gazed into her sweet green eyes and my world shifted.

"Is the eclipse still there?" I asked out shakily, weak from my labor.

"Yes," replied Lucien. "It looks like she's the 'little omega' now," He teased. I smiled at his joke, but my heart worried about her future already.

"I'm not giving her up to the omega nest when she's twelve, no matter how much money they offer me," I whispered fiercely, hugging her close to my chest.

"We'll do everything in our power to ensure she remains with us," Kayden vowed solemnly, stroking my sweat-soaked hair.

I had a tiny omega daughter now, and it was up to me to protect her and give her the life she deserved. I gazed up around me at the four fierce alphas by my side, and I knew she was going to be just fine.

THE END

Read on to **Book 2**: Alpha's Fated Desire, featuring the compassionate, mysterious blonde, Gabriella, from the omega stage at the Were gathering. Who will be her pack of fated mates? Or will she be doomed to remain at gatherings after gatherings, forever unmated?

Thank you so much for reading!

Thank you so much for reading!

Please leave a review, letting me know what you think.

It helps authors like me keep producing more stories for you.

For any questions about the story, please email: author.mina.summers@gmail.com

Join my newsletter here for updates on my next story.

Find me on Instagram: @author_mina.summers

Find me on Tiktok: @author_mina.summers

Don't miss out on Gabriella's story here!

Made in United States
Orlando, FL
16 January 2024

42592294R00140